THE
GHOST
DANCE
CAPER

Also by Monica Hughes

MONICA HUGHES

THE
GHOST
DANCE
CAPER

Stoddart

Published in 1993 by
Stoddart Publishing Co. Limited
34 Lesmill Road
Toronto, Canada
M3B 2T6
(416) 445-3333

First published in Great Britain in 1978 by
Hamish Hamilton Children's Books Limited.

Methuen paperback edition published in 1986.

Canadian Cataloguing in Publication Data

Hughes, Monica, 1925–
The ghost dance caper

ISBN 0-7736-7407-1

I. Title.

PS8565.U43G56 1993   jC813'.54   C93-094987-0
PZ7.H83Gh 1993

Cover Design: Brant Cowie/Artplus Limited
Cover illustration: Deborah and Allan Drew-Brook-Cormack

Printed and bound in the United States of America

*Stoddart Publishing gratefully acknowledges the support of the
Canada Council, Ontario Ministry of Culture, Tourism, and
Recreation, Ontario Arts Council, and Ontario Publishing Centre
in the development of writing and publishing in Canada.*

For those people who have
found their Spirit. And for those
who are searching.

The description of the Blackfoot Ghost Dance ceremony and the myths relating to it are taken from "Blackfoot Ghost Dance" by Hugh A. Dempsey, published by the Glenbow-Alberta Institute as an occasional paper.

The description of the 'sweat' was inspired by an article by Jim Davies in the Edmonton Journal, *January 31, 1976: "To Great Spirit through Heat".*

Chapter One

Sundays were the good days. Every Sunday Tom's father drove him out to the reservation to visit his great-grandfather. He looked forward to it all week, though not to the argument that preceded it, starting as a low grumble every Saturday and peaking at the breakfast table on Sunday morning.

"Why will you never listen to me, Mark? I'm concerned about Tom's future. I don't think the boy should be spending all his time out there." Whenever this argument began his parents would talk about Tom as if he were suddenly invisible.

"For Pete's sake, Carol, once a week isn't all the time. You know how important it is to the old man." Tom's father always called Chief Samuel Lightfoot 'the old man' when he was talking about him, though he was very polite to his face. Why not "grandfather", Tom wondered, for the thousandth time. You'd think Dad would be as proud as could be to have a real honest-to-goodness Indian chief as a grandfather.

"I've got relatives too, you know," his mother snapped back. "They'd be very happy to have Tom visit them once in a while."

"For crying out loud, Carol, you haven't a relative closer than the Manitoba border."

"Well, at least you could have your grandfather visit *here*, instead of Tom going out *there* all the time." *There* was the reservation. Tom noticed that it was a word Mother didn't use, any more

1

than Dad liked to say 'grandfather'.

"You know I've asked him, Carol. He won't come. He doesn't care for the city."

"Well, I just don't like Tom going out there so often, and if you'd pay attention to the boy, Mark, you'd see it yourself. The old man fills him full of stories and he comes home in a daze with his mind filled with crazy dreams, and it takes him half the week to settle down to school again. Have you seen the grades he's been getting?"

Tom slouched down in his chair and tried to think himself invisible. It was horrible being argued over, like two dogs with a bone. Sometimes he panicked and thought that maybe he was breaking up their marriage. Arguments over him seemed to be happening all the time nowadays. But today was all right. Dad was in a sunny mood.

"Give him time, Carol. He'll settle down. It's only October. It always takes a while after summer vacation to pick up good study habits. But he'll do it, won't you, son?"

Tom slid back off his spine and sat up. He nodded and tried to look intelligent without committing himself.

"I had straight A's right through school," Dad went on. Tom turned his mind off again. He'd heard this story an awful lot of times recently too. "It takes brains and plenty of hard work to become a lawyer, Tom. I had to claw my way up every inch, with nobody to help me. It'll be different for you, son. As soon as you've got your degree you'll come into my law office, and from there on it'll be a clear road to success."

2

"I don't know that I want to be a lawyer, Dad." Tom just wasn't thinking, or he'd never have let the words out, though they'd been on his mind all summer.

His mother put her tea-cup down with a tiny crash. "You *see*, Mark? That's what I mean. We've given him everything, every possible advantage a boy could have . . . you see? It's your grandfather again, putting ideas into his head." She flushed with vexation.

Tom looked like his father, all Indian. His skin was a smoky brown, his eyes so dark as to be almost black above his high cheek bones, and his hair, which his mother made him cut short, as if she were ashamed of it, was blue-black and as straight as a string. When Tom or his father got mad their faces just got a little darker and their black eyes smouldered. But Mother, with her fair skin and pale eyes, went bright pink. He could see the blood now, slowly rising in her neck and ears and along her jaw-line. Her eyes got pink too and watery. Tom looked down at his plate and busily buttered his toast. It was embarrassing when Mother showed her feelings that way, almost like seeing her with no clothes on.

"Let it be, Carol," Dad growled. "It's just growing pains. He'll be a lawyer all right, don't worry. What else?"

His mother flounced out of the breakfast room with an angry snort, ending the argument for that particular week.

An hour later, on the front seat of his father's Lincoln Continental, Tom leaned back and

3

stretched contentedly. He felt the bothers of the previous week slowly peel off him, layer by layer, like the skin of an onion, as the kilometres flicked by. The highway was crowded. Everyone else seemed to be escaping today, making one last trip to the lake, tidying up their cabins and making the most of the good weather before winter set in.

The stands of poplar were gold against the dark green of spruce and pine. Overhead the sky was perfectly empty, a newly washed blue-green. Tom's spirits rose higher and higher as they turned off the highway and bumped along the dirt road that led through the reservation.

Great-grandfather was standing at the door of his two-room house, on the look-out for them, the way he always was on Sunday mornings, his eyes narrowed against the sun.

"Good morning, Grandfather. How've you been?"

"Morning, Mark. Fine, fine. What about you? You look tired."

"Been a tough week."

"Spend the day with Tom and me and unwind a little."

"Thanks, Grandfather, but I'm playing golf with Judge Bates at ten. I'd better be moving or I'll be late."

Every week it was the same ritual, word for word. Dad waved and smiled broadly at them both as he turned the car. But his eyes didn't smile, Tom noticed. They looked desperate, like the eyes of a trapped rabbit.

The old man raised his hand in acknowledg-

4

ment, slowly, like a blessing, Tom thought. He didn't smile back. His face was grave, carved out of mahogany in deep lines and furrows. Tom stood close to him, and together they watched the big car fish-tail impatiently down the curved road, leaving a plume of white dust in the air behind it.

The old man put his hand on Tom's shoulder. "Tea first, eh? And then ...?"

"A tramp through the bush, please, Great-grandfather." The week's load of math, social studies, language, kids and teachers fell from Tom's shoulders. He gave a huge contented sigh and followed his great-grandfather into the house.

Tea was brewed in the kettle, strong and sweet, a brew from another world. It had nothing in common with the ceremony of Mother's drawing room, with the Royal Worcester tea service, cups as translucent as egg-shells and as easily breakable, the tea pale and faintly aromatic.

Great-grandfather's tea had ceremony too. He poured it from the kettle in careful silence. He put in the sugar and stirred it four times, the number sacred to the four cardinal points, as he had taught Tom. He raised the coffee-mug — he'd bought them at three for a dollar with a tankful of gas at the service station — and drank slowly, breathing in the hot steam with the liquid in a satisfying 'shoosh'. Tom copied him happily.

At home Mother would say "If you can't drink a cup of tea like a gentleman you'd better have it in the kitchen", and he would slink away, ashamed and yet relieved. Here he sucked away and smiled across the kitchen table at Great-grandfather, and

5

watched Great-grandfather smile slowly back. It was a marvellous smile, that broke the long grooves of the old man's face into a thousand horizontal wrinkles. His back teeth were gone, but his front ones were straight and strong, a little yellowed with tea and tobacco. It was a smile that was as warm as a hug.

Tom looked lovingly around the room, at the old linoleum on the floor, the family snapshots in their cheap frames, the sagging sofa in front of the stove. If only Mother and Dad would let themselves be part of this too. But imagining them sitting at the table, he suddenly saw the room through his mother's eyes.

"Why don't you brighten the place up a bit, Great-grandfather? I could help."

"Get a genuine Indian blanket maybe, and hang a war bonnet on the wall." The old chief's face smiled in a thousand tissue paper creases. "You've been listening to your mother, Tom. That's not Indian, all that. Indian is inside yourself. How you feel, not what you hang on your walls. Or maybe you'd like it better if I went up into the foothills and set up my tipi there."

Tom's face lit up. "Gosh, Great-grandfather, that'd be super."

"Think your mother would let you go all that way every Sunday? Or let you sleep out in the wilderness?"

"She might."

"No, Tom. She's made up her mind and your father's too. She'll never let him head back to the tipi, nor you either. I don't blame her, mind you.

She's done very well for my grandson. I know that that big house and all the fine furniture in it are mostly her doing."

"I have to wipe my feet all the time." Tom's voice asked for sympathy.

"And so you do here. This may be only linoleum. But it's my home, and you don't bring dirt in here either. You through with your tea yet?"

Tom swigged the rest of the hot sweet brew, and together they walked out the back door through the old chief's bedroom, and past the out-house and up the hill. Beyond the scrubby hill, where a few bony cows grazed and the pump of an oil-rig nodded ceaselessly up and down, was a fold of aspen-covered parkland, and beyond it the densely wooded bluffs above the river.

They walked in comfortable silence, Great-grandfather's moccasins silent even on the fallen leaves, Tom in his runners trying to walk as quietly on the crackling golden carpet. They stopped for a family of ground squirrels and a fat woodchuck gathering winter fodder, and they watched a pair of magpies walk across the grass in front of them, as bold as brass, sweeping their blue and black tail feathers as if they were royalty.

At the top of the bluffs the trees ceased and the grass grew sparse and dry. They squatted near the edge where they could look down fifty or sixty feet to the river. There was a faint breeze, smelling of woodsmoke and bitter fall leaves. Sitting close to Great-grandfather Tom could also smell his special smell, tobacco, his deer-skin coat, and the stuff he greased his hair with before he smoothed it back to braid. He leaned against Great-grandfather's shoulder and sniffed in the familiar scent, his eyes half closed against the sun, and he wished that Sunday could could go on for ever.

"Something bothering you, boy?"

"Yeah. I guess."

"Want to talk about it?"

"I dunno." Tom stirred restlessly and stared down at the river, milky with glacial silt. The old man sat motionless as a statue, as waiting and accepting as the rocks of the bluffs.

After a while Tom blurted out, "I'm in Grade Nine this year, Great-grandfather. High school next year. I have to make up my mind which courses I'm going to take. I have to know what I want to be."

"You're thirteen years old now, Tom?" The old man's voice was still the voice of a chief, full of quiet authority, though it was no longer resonant, but whispery, like autumn leaves. A fall voice, a winter voice.

"Yes. I'll be fourteen in January."

"Almost a man." The voice was matter of fact.

Tom's eyes flew to his face. *A man,* he thought, startled. "I am?" he said aloud. "I don't feel like a man. I don't even know who I am, Great-grandfather. How'm I going to decide on a career that I'm going to be stuck with for the rest of my life when I don't even know who I am? It doesn't make sense." He stared up into the old chief's face. Behind the wrinkles and the stained teeth was something rock-hard, certain. "Great-grandfather, help me."

The old man nodded, not a passing nod, but formally, as if he were accepting a commitment. Nothing was said for a long time. The shadows slid around to their left. The sun sparkled down on the river . . .

"What does your father want?"

"For me to be a lawyer like him. He simply can't imagine me doing anything else."

"He's a very successful one, I hear."

"Mother says he's likely to be made a judge pretty soon. I think that's why he goes in for politics and playing golf with all those important people on Sundays. I'm sure he doesn't really like it."

"And what does you mother want for you? Do you know that?"

"For me to be a success. Lawyer, doctor, whatever. Just as long as I'm successful."

"What about you, Tom? Is that what you want — success?"

"Not as a lawyer or a doctor, that's for sure. Why, I'd be trapped in school for another ten or twelve years, what with university and post-grad. Twelve years, before I could even get started. Then suppose I hated it? There's got to be some other kind of success. Look at you, Great-grandfather. You're successful."

The sun reflected off the broken lines of the old man's face as he threw back his head and laughed. "You want to be a successful Indian chief, boy? That's one thing you can't have." His face grew still again. "My son left the reserve. That was his choice, and before he died in the war he made

9

enough money to give your father a good education. Your father married a white girl and chose the white man's world to live in. He hewed a new path through the forest for his family, and it is on that path that your feet are placed."

"But I don't want it!"

"What do you want?"

"I don't know. I don't know anything. I don't even know if I'm really white or Indian."

"Which do you feel?"

"Neither. Both. Muddled, I guess. When I'm out here with you I feel so good, but all the time part of me knows that it's not really real, it's like a holiday, and the other world is waiting for me back in the city. Mother, Dad, school, all that."

"Is school so bad?"

"Not all the time. Sometimes it's really interesting, and I feel part of what's going on, and I do have some friends. But then something happens. One of the teachers or maybe a kid makes a crack about Indians, and right away I'm boiling mad, and I feel all Indian and I just wish I could scalp them or something."

The old chief laughed. "That's not the way, Tom, and you know it. So you feel mixed up. Well, I can understand that. You stand between two worlds with a foot in each. It is no wonder you feel uncomfortable. If it were only fifty, a hundred years ago, I would send you off into the mountains to find your spirit. That is what you are really searching for. A spirit to guide your steps through life, to show you the direction it is meant for you to take."

"Find my spirit? Tell me how?"

"I have told you the story before. I'm sure I have."

"Not since I was little. It wouldn't have been important then. Tell it to me now, please."

The old man settled himself comfortably, cross-legged on the short dry grass, and he looked up the milky river as if he were reading the past.

"Long, long ago," he began, and Tom lay back on the turf with a contented sigh and looked up into the intense blue of the fall sky. His great-grandfather's voice came to him soft and sing-song, mixed up with the hum of a late bee in the clover . . .

"Long before the treaty was signed and the railway came, long before I was born, our people roamed the plains from here to the Rockies. And every summer the buffalo came out of the south, thousand upon thousand of them, so that the whole plain was dark with them and their hooves were like a never-ending thunder to the ears. To our people they gave everything that was necessary for life, meat to eat, skins for clothing and tipis, bones and sinews for weapons and tools, dung for our fires. Their yearly coming gave meaning and shape to the life of the Blackfoot people.

"But a man needs something beyond that, something that is personal to himself. So when it happened that a youth arrived at that time when he began to ask himself 'Who am I?' and 'What is the meaning of my life? What am I here for?', then he would seek out a spirit to guide him throughout his life, to give him direction, and to be his help in time of trouble or danger.

"The spirit might come to him as a hawk, and by studying its swiftness, its patience and keenness of eye, the young man might learn to become a mighty hunter. Or perhaps the spirit would come to him as a rabbit, teaching him that in stillness there may be safety, or if stillness fails there is speed. But whatever spirit appeared to the young man, that spirit he would adopt, so that it might guide him throughout his life."

"But how would he find it?"

"You know, Tom. I have told you before, when you were small."

"Tell me again," Tom urged, and the old man's sing-song voice took up the old story.

"The young man would leave his people and go away alone, taking with him neither food nor water. He would climb to a high place and there he would remain, praying and waiting, for a spirit to come to him. He might see his spirit the first night, or he might have to wait two, three or even four nights. Even then the spirit might not come to him and he would have to return to his people ashamed, still a boy, unguided and purposeless. Or, worse still, he might become afraid of the night people, the ghosts of the dead, the *sipi-i-tapi*, and run back to the tent of his family without even waiting for the spirit to come to him all the long, long distance from the land of the dead, the land of the night people."

"So what could he do?"

"The young man, or someone in his family, would seek out a wise man in the tribe who owned a ghost bundle, and he would say to him, 'Arrange a ghost dance for me so that I may be protected from the night people when I go up alone into the high places to find my spirit.' Then the man who owned the ghost bundle would arrange a ghost dance, and everyone who was close to the young man would be there. Then the wise man would pray to the spirits of the youth's ancestors and the spirits of all the dead owners of the ghost bundle, that they might come and protect him from all the other spirits who crowd the night paths, so that they might not snatch the young man's mind out of his body. Then there would be a dance and feasting, though the owner of the bundle and the young man would not eat, but instead take the sweat. After that the young man would slip away alone to find his spirit, knowing that he was safely protected."

"Maybe I should go away and find my spirit."

"Without the ghost dance I do not think it is possible. The way my father told it to me, the two go together, the dance and the spirit seeking."

"Then let's put on a ghost dance. You could, couldn't you, Great-grandfather? You're chief."

"We have no bundle." The old man's head dropped as if he were ashamed. "All those things have gone. The bundles were sold by those who had no right to sell them to those who had no right to buy. It is lost, all lost. Even the memory of the dance and the prayers slip away from me. They are no more than faint memories, like the taste of my mother's milk."

"Then I'll watch for my spirit without the ghost

dance. I'm not afraid of the dark, anyway."

"Maybe you should be. A wise man knows what he should be afraid of."

"It's all different nowadays. I mean, the night is full of noise and lights now. There are street lights and cars. It's different from when you were a boy."

"If the night people do not prowl any longer for the minds of living men, then I think maybe the spirits we seek have left too."

"When I was little I was afraid of the dark."

"Maybe you were smarter then."

"Maybe. Great-grandfather, what does a ghost bundle look like?"

"Like any other bundle."

"What's inside it?"

"What is inside a bundle we do not talk of, and they are unwrapped only during the ceremony." The old man's voice was serious, almost reproving.

"But . . ."

"They are what they are. A cloth of buffalo skin coloured with red ochre and containing all the sacred things that are necessary for the dance. So you might have a tobacco bundle, a buffalo bundle, a sun-dance bundle . . ."

"And a ghost bundle. Only I do wish I knew what was inside it. Maybe we could reconstruct one."

"No. Even I cannot tell you. Only if you were to witness the dance would you see the things that are used. But that can never be. The bundles are all lost. And what is in them is gone from our minds." The old chief made a gesture, cutting the air with

14

the side of his hand like a knife.

"Why red ochre? On the bundle, I mean."

"Because red ochre is sacred to the Indian peoples."

"Why?"

"Because it has always been so." The old man began to laugh. "You ask so many questions, Tom, maybe you had better be a lawyer after all!"

Chapter Two

Tom began to settle down in school again. It had felt as if the kids were all peas of different sizes being shaken up and graded in a sieve. During those first weeks there had been new looks, a new timetable, new faces. Then suddenly a day came when it all seemed to fall into place, and Tom knew where he was supposed to be and what he was supposed to be doing on any particular day from eight-thirty to the final bell at three.

They got shaken up and sorted out into friends, enemies and neutrals. Tom found he had fewer enemies and more neutrals this year. There were three boys he liked well enough to invite to sleep over at his house and work on his railway and model rockets, and be invited back to sleep at their houses.

There was one real friend too this year, and that made all the difference. Pete Cummings was a person he could talk to about things that mattered, private things. He was new to the school, a skinny sharp-faced fourteen year old, in the top rank of every class. Not that he played up to the teachers. In fact he had a streak of lawlessness in him and a love of practical jokes that was always getting him into trouble. Only, being Pete, he could talk his way out again.

It wasn't long before Tom found himself telling Pete everything about Great-grandfather and the spirits and the ghost bundle. Pete didn't even crack a smile and when Tom had finished he said, "It's too bad we don't know where all the bundles have got to. If we only did we could steal them back."

"Steal?" Tom stared.

"Not really steal. Repossess. Nations do it all the time with pieces of territory and works of art. And just look at the crusaders and the Holy Land. They went on killing each other for years over that."

"You make it sound so logical, Pete. But I don't even know where the bundles went to. They could even be destroyed. I mean, this was fifty, even a hundred years ago."

"I suppose we could ask Mr Miles if he's ever heard of any." Mr Miles was the social studies teacher.

"You've got to be joking! You've seen him pick on me. He hates Indians. Anyway, I don't think he'd know. Everything he teaches us he gets right out of the book."

Tom forgot about that conversation, but he couldn't forget what Great-grandfather had said about searching for his spirit, and secretly he tried to fast and keep a nightly vigil. It wasn't easy. He had to pretend that he'd had supper over at a friend's house. Then, after he'd gone to bed, his stomach growling emptily, he'd force himself to stay awake until the sounds of his parents had died away and the house was quiet. Then he'd sneak down the passage and climb on a chair to shin himself up into the attic.

It was the highest place in the house, and it was certainly uncomfortable enough to qualify as a test, Tom thought. He had to sit on a joist, praying he didn't fall asleep and roll off and crash through the ceiling into the passage below. It was dark, so pitch-black that sometimes he felt he was going blind. When the moon shone he could see just a glimmer of light through the ventilation louvres at the end of the roof. But once the moon had moved around there was nothing. It was totally silent too. Up at the top of the house he couldn't hear the whisper of the furnace fan or the hum of the refrigerator motor.

He stuck it out for three nights, but the only thing that happened was that he fell asleep during French, and caught a cold from sitting up all night in an unheated attic. He didn't tell Pete about that. He felt too stupid.

Near the end of October, Grade Nine had their first field trip. They'd been studying the colonization of Alberta and they got to spend a noisy afternoon in the pioneer gallery of the Provincial Museum. It wasn't bad, lots of interesting junk. Close to the main entrance of the gallery was a display of Victorian music boxes, and jukeboxes and 'mechanical orchestras' of the early twenties. Their guide demonstrated some of them, and all the girls put their hands over their ears and screeched at the tinny noise. The boys didn't hand around long. There was a big display of vintage cars just around the corner.

When Mr Miles called them they clattered down the marble stairs in a noisy throng. At the bottom Pete nudged Tom in the ribs.

"Quit shoving," said Tom and punched him back in a friendly way.

"No, seriously. Look over there." He pointed. At the bottom of the staircase was a big archway leading to another gallery. BLACKFOOT CULTURE it announced in big modern letters above the entrance. "Have you ever been in there?"

"No. Have you?"

"Not yet. Want to go?"

"Why not? We've spent all afternoon looking at early colonial whats-its."

"Artifacts."

"We might as well look at my people's artifacts too. After all, they were here first."

They dodged across the marble-floored concourse and through the arch, followed by the other boys, ripe for mischief. Soon there were a dozen kids milling about, exclaiming at the chiefs' and braves' clothing, and the embroidery on their leggings and saddles. Some of the boys started a game of dodge around the tipi display in the middle of the gallery, and it wasn't long before one of them gave an ululating cry and another responded with a war whoop and a Hollywood version of Indian dancing.

Tom flushed angrily and turned away to glare through the glass at the dusty exhibits in a case tucked away in the farthest corner of the room. Idly he began to read the labels.

When Mr Miles hurried into the gallery to scold the students and line them up for their return to the bus, Tom didn't even turn round. He stared into the dusty cabinet as if he were hypnotised.

"Come on, Tom." Pete jabbed him in the ribs. "Hey, what's the matter with you? Are you sick or something? Tom!"

Tom turned and stared blankly at Pete as if he'd never seen him before. Then he blinked and licked his lips. "Pete, look over there in the corner. Am I seeing things? Read what it says."

"We're going to miss the bus and Mr Miles will have our hide. Oh, all right. I'll think of a good alibi. Now where do you mean?"

His eyes followed the direction of Tom's shaking finger, past spotted sepia photographs of old ceremonies and dusty red packets, some of them closed, some opened to disclose motley collections of pebbles, bones, berries, grass and feathers.

GHOST BUNDLE
Only known example of this ceremonial bundle
Recently donated to the Provincial Museum
by the heirs of the Strathmore Estate.

Tucked away in the farthest corner of the cabinet was an unopened bundle, bound with a thong.

"Holy cow!" Pete pushed his nose against the glass and stared. "Wow! No wonder you were in a spin, Tom. That's fantastic. Hey, Tom, are you all right? You look most peculiar."

Tom stared blankly. "What?"

"Oh, come on. We'll talk later. Pull yourself together." Pete hauled Tom by the arm out of the gallery and across the concourse. Their class had already filled the bus and Mr Miles was on his way back to look for them.

"There you are, you two. I might have known it. Come on, hurry it up."

"Tom feels sick, sir. Maybe I could walk him home. He'd be better off in the fresh air. I mean, you never know."

Mr Miles hesitated, looking from Tom's face to the crowded bus. "Will your mother be home?"

"Yes, sir. I think so."

"I'll phone and tell her to expect you early. No loitering, mind."

He bustled over to the information desk. The security man pointed to the cloakroom area. Mr Miles tutted and turned to Tom and Pete. "Sit," he commanded as if he were training a dog. "I'll be back in a moment."

He bustled over to the pay phone in the cloakroom. Tom sat with the same blank expression on his face. Pete's was alive with curiosity, which he wiped out as Mr Miles came back, replacing it with an expression of willing concern.

"All right. Take him directly home, Cummings. No larking about, now."

"Yes, sir. No, sir. Don't worry, sir."

They watched him go. "Now," said Pete as soon as they were alone. "Just go on sitting there for a minute and tell me why you've gone so peculiar."

Tom found himself explaining in a shaking voice about the attic vigil and the skipped meals, and about how none of it was any good anyway.

"Well, I'm not surprised, the way you went about it," said Pete briskly. "I don't understand the necessity for all this spirit searching business, but if it's that important we'd better go ahead and do it right. Meanwhile have a chocolate bar. You could get really ill not eating."

"What do you mean 'do it right'?" Tom wolfed down the chocolate. "Gosh, this is good. Sure you can spare it all?"

"I mean all this hanging around in draughty attics is stupidly unscientific. No wonder you've got a cold. If you're really going through with this spirit search then you've got to do it properly. We've got to get hold of that ghost bundle and take it to your great-grandfather and have him put on the dance. Then you ask *his* advice as to the best place to wait for your spirit to come."

Tom stared blankly at Pete. "Huh? Get the ghost bundle? How?"

"Rip it off, of course. It'll be a terrific caper."

"*Steal* the bundle? But ... I mean ... it's illegal."

"Don't get so technical. What's the matter with you? We went into all this ages ago. Remember what your great-grandfather said? They had no right to sell it and the Strathmore people had no right to buy it. Anyway, it's like we were saying, countries do it all the time. They call it ... what's the word? ... repatriating. Well, that's just what we're going to do with the ghost bundle. We're going to repatriate it to the Blackfoot people."

"We?"

"You're not going to keep me out of it, are you? I mean, let's face it, Tom, you're okay, but honestly I don't think you've got enough brains to break into a museum and get away without being caught. It'll be a terrific lark. I've always wanted to do something like this, but the right opportunity's never come along."

"I suppose you can help if you're sure you want to. But still . . . stealing from the museum . . . Pete, are you sure we should? I mean . . . you know Dad's a lawyer. They're considering him for a judge. If anything went wrong and we were caught . . ."

"Put yourself in my hands and you won't get caught, I promise you. Tell you what, think about it for a couple of days, okay? Only stop this vigil nonsense and start eating and sleeping properly. You're going to need all your endurance and cunning when we come to the vital moment."

Tom looked sideways at his friend as they walked home together. Was Pete kidding? With his academic manner and the words he used, it wasn't always easy to tell. Did he honestly mean them to rob the museum, or was it just another of Pete's leg-pulls?

Pete was right about one thing. The bundle didn't really belong to the museum at all. If it belonged anywhere it was with Chief Samuel Lightfoot and his people. "I suppose we could ask the museum people if they'd let us have it back? If we were to explain . . ." he suggested diffidently.

"You have to be joking! We'd never even get past the security guard to talk to the top man. You know how adults treat us. We wouldn't be taken seriously for a moment. And don't forget, if we *did* express an interest in the bundle and then we took it, they'd know just where to look, wouldn't they? No, Tom, we've got to take the initiative and do the appropriating ourselves. Honestly, I don't see what you're worried about. They probably won't even miss it. That was the tackiest display case —

all dusty too, did you notice? I bet if we took out the bundle and the label, and then just moved the rest of the stuff over slightly to hide the gap, they'd never notice it was gone. Not ever."

Tom thought about it for the next two days. He noticed Pete looking at him once or twice in a questioning sort of way, but nothing was said on the subject until they were leaving school on Friday afternoon. Then all Pete said was "Well?" in such an unpestering kind of way that Tom began to feel that his objections were most unreasonable.

"I don't know. It depends on what sort of plan you've got," he hedged uneasily. "I really meant it about Dad, Pete. If anything got in the way of his being made a judge it would be the absolute end of everything. He'd probably never speak to me again, and I wouldn't blame him. Things are rough enough at home already."

"It won't happen. Stop worrying. We won't jump in unprepared. In fact tomorrow I want to go down to the museum and scout out the lay of the land. Are you game?"

"Sure. I guess so. So long as I'm not committed to anything, not till we've seen what it's like."

"I'll meet you there at ten. Don't be late."

Next morning the two of them strolled in a casual fashion into the Blackfoot gallery. Pete made no attempt to approach the little cabinet in the corner until the room was empty. Then he strolled over, calling to Tom, "Come and look at this junk." As Tom came up he whispered, "Cover me. I want to check how the case fastens without the TV camera noticing."

His hand flashed over the lock. There was a scratching sound, followed by a click, and then another click. Pete turned casually away, pocketing a penknife. "Rotten little lock," he muttered. "You could open it with a toothpick."

"Where did you learn a trick like that?" Tom gasped.

"Suppose I told you in the deepest confidence that my father is a master spy."

"I'd say you were a liar."

"Doubting Thomas. That's why I've changed schools so often. I'm his cover, you see." He looked casually around the room. "There's only one TV snoop in here. Should be easy to avoid if we check its timing carefully."

Tom looked uneasily up at the small camera near the ceiling in one corner of the room. It rotated with a clockwork mechanism, its 'eye' scanning the room from left to right and back again.

"There are no windows in the gallery," Pete said thoughtfully, "And we certainly can't use the emergency exit. You can see the alarm system from here."

"Then it's no good." Tom tried to keep the relief out of his voice.

"I didn't say that. Don't give up so easily. Nothing ventured, nothing gained. I've got an idea . . ." Tom saw with dread the sparkle in his friend's eye. "I've got it. Simplicity itself. We'll get ourselves locked in at closing time. Then we don't have to worry about breaking in. As soon as it's quite dark and peaceful I'll unlock the cabinet, we grab the

25

bundle and dive straight out those doors." Pete pointed at the emergency exit. It was marked with a red light and a large notice across the push-bar.

DO NOT TOUCH
This door activates the alarm system.
For emergency use only.

He giggled suddenly, abandoning his scholarly manner. "It'll be an emergency all right."

Tom found himself giggling too. Then he sobered up. "Look, Pete, that's all very well, but what about the notice? There'll be alarm bells ringing, and guards and police..."

"The whole point is that they're all going to think that it's a break-in. They'll be searching *inside* the museum for the burglar, and by the time they look outside we'll be long gone. I tell you what, let's go outside right now and scout around this side of the building to find the neatest way of getting clear of the grounds. Okay?"

"I guess so." Tom had the dizzy feeling that he was trapped on a giant roller-coaster. It was wildly exciting, and yet a part of him wished he were back on firm ground again. Only how could he back out now without being chicken?

He followed the eager Pete outside. It was easy to work out that the emergency exit from the Blackfoot gallery must be the one that faced the driveway on the west side of the building.

"It's awfully public," Tom said dubiously.

"Not when it's dark." Pete's sharp eyes flashed around. "No good going south. When the parking lot's empty a person would be more noticeable than usual. And Second Avenue is the first place anyone would look when they heard the alarm. I wonder what's on the other side of that hedge . . ."

He dashed across the driveway. "Look. It's one of those fancy crescents overlooking the river. It'll be a cinch. We'd be around the bend in less than a minute. Even if they cordoned off the area and searched the streets we'd look perfectly innocent."

"Cordon? Search? Pete, let's not. Let's forget the whole thing, huh?"

"Don't *worry*. It's not going to happen. I'm just being prepared for all eventualities, like any smart spy."

"I don't like it." Tom was abrupt.

"I don't see why. It'll go like clockwork, I promise you." Pete stared, and Tom saw his face change. "You're not going to chicken out on me, are you? I mean, the whole caper is in aid of you, you realise that?"

Tom swallowed. Pete was the first really good friend he'd ever had in school. "Of course I'm not chickening out. It's just that . . . well, I don't think you plan's perfect, that's all. For instance, suppose the police should get to the museum really fast, before we've had time to get around the crescent?"

Pete's face relaxed and he nodded thoughtfully. "Not bad. We'll make a master spy out of you yet. First point, we'll time our get-away. You go and stand on Second Avenue. Stroll up and down or something, but keep your eye on your watch, because in sixty seconds from when I say the alarm's going to go off."

"What!"

"Not really, you idiot. Just a dry run. Anyway, at the sixty second mark sprint towards the driveway and see if you can see me anywhere."

"That'll be easy. Bet I do."

"Bet you don't. Now, go!"

Pete strolled away from Tom, skinny and arrogant. He crossed the lawn to the west exit, looking as if he owned the place. Tom watched him enviously, wishing he could walk that way and be that sure of himself. Then as Pete waved he remembered what he was supposed to be doing and dashed out onto the avenue fronting the museum, one eye on the sweep second of his watch. Virtuously he turned his back and waited.

It touched the sixty-second mark and he sprinted back to the museum driveway. Pete was nowhere in sight. He scanned the hedge and the parking lot. Then he sprinted back to the avenue and along the crescent that ran along the western boundary of the museum grounds. It was empty too.

He was standing uncertainly on the corner when Pete came into view, strolling along the avenue towards him from the west.

"Well?" Pete's face was flushed and triumphant, and there were dead leaves and twigs in his hair.

"It works," Tom admitted. "But I don't see how you did it."

"I just went through that hedge like a rabbit. There are lots of gaps at the bottom. Then I strolled up the crescent and out at the other end."

"Your hair looks as if you fell out of a tree."

Pete brushed it off. "Yes, we'll have to remember to tidy ourselves up. And we need one more touch. Something to make us look so innocent that nobody would even think of asking us what we were doing." He frowned for a minute, absently picking dead leaves and bark out of his hair. Then his face cleared and he began to chuckle. "Perfect."

"What?"

"Super alibi. But I'm going to keep it for a surprise. Trust me."

"That's what you keep saying," Tom grumbled.

"Have I ever let you down?"

"I haven't known you that long, and I've never been on a caper like this with you before."

"Something new every day. Now look." Pete's voice became business-like. "We've got to go back to the museum and scout around for a good place to hide. Come on."

"I don't think we're going to have much choice, if any."

"Don't be so negative. Obviously we want to find somewhere as close as possible to the Blackfoot gallery, but we might as well be thorough and go over the whole place, keeping our eyes open and our mouths shut. After all, we don't want to tip our hand to the security guards, do we? Then we'll pick up something to eat in the cafeteria and go outside to compare notes. All right?"

Tom nodded and they set off. The museum was packed, even for a Saturday, and the boys followed the crowd up the stairs and into one of the special galleries.

OPENING TODAY: *Pre-Columbian Art, on loan*

from the Museum of Mexico the sign said.

"Might as well see what the fuss is about, I suppose," Pete said, elbowing his way through the crowd, Tom at his heels.

Heavy glass cases around the walls and on stands in the centre of the small room held collections of small carvings, none of them bigger than Tom's fist. But . . . "Wow!" He pressed his nose against the glass until it steamed over. "They're all solid gold!" He stared until the person behind him jabbed him in the ribs with his elbow and he had to move on.

After they had disentangled themselves from the crowd they walked around the other galleries, keeping their eyes open and their mouths shut, the way Pete had said. The whole time Pete's face had a brooding look. Tom was beginning to dread that look. It usually meant more complications.

"Piece of luck that exhibit being on just now," Pete said thoughtfully.

Tom stopped dead in the middle of the concourse. "Pete, you wouldn't! Would you?"

"Idiot!" Pete cuffed him on the head. "What do you think I am, some sort of criminal? Danger, yes. Vice, never! No, you nut, what I was thinking was that the security people will be sweating blood over that exhibition. It must be worth an absolute fortune. And so portable too. Not like that silver nugget they had a while back, remember, that four men couldn't even lift. You mark my words, all the attention's going to be on that gallery upstairs. Nobody's going to fuss about some dusty old Indian artifacts that aren't worth a cent."

"Thanks a lot!" Tom cuffed him back, and they scuffled their way down the passage to the cafeteria, stocked up on potato chips and soft drinks and took it all outdoors and across the lawns to where they could sit comfortably, their backs against a tree, with a clear view around and no chance of anyone sneaking up and eavesdropping on them.

"Well?" said Pete.

"Well, yourself! I couldn't see anywhere to hide. In movies there is always a janitor's cleaning room or a big closet. There just doesn't seem to be anything like that around, not out in the open where we could get at it anyway. This museum is too modern, that's the trouble. Another thing, Pete, I don't a bit like the idea of crossing that marble floor of the concourse in the middle of the night. It echoes like crazy, did you notice? You might as well advertise."

"I agree with you a hundred percent."

"You *do*?"

"So that leaves the Blackfoot gallery itself."

"There's nowhere to hide in *there*."

"Sure there is. Two places, in fact. We could pretend to be Indian braves in the wax-work display, or we could hide inside the tipi."

"We'd look pretty stupid running up Second Avenue in buckskin and beads, not to mention war paint."

"True. Which leaves the tipi."

"We couldn't hide in there, Pete. We'd be noticed right away. It'd be the first place a guard would look."

"If he were searching for someone, I agree. But he won't be. Not really. He'll just be walking smartly around the museum, once an hour or whatever it is. Then he's going to race back upstairs and count the gold statues again. I bet you anything we'd never be noticed."

"I'm not about to take you up on that. If I win we end up in jail. It's a rotten bet."

"We won't. Let's test it out. I'll come back this afternoon just before closing time, and I'll drop a dollar bill on the floor behind the Indian figures around the fire in the tipi. While I'm at it I'll hang around and see how the guards go about clearing the galleries at closing time. Then tomorrow we'll come back and see if the dollar is still there."

"Sundays I go out to Great-grandfather's."

"So you do. All right. I'll come back myself as soon as the place opens."

"I don't see that dropping a dollar on the floor really proves anything. We're a darn sight larger than a dollar bill and much harder to hide."

"I'm not going to *hide* it. That's the whole point. I'll just lay it down in the middle of the floor in the roped-off area behind the display by the fireplace. If it's still there tomorrow it'll mean that the guard just pokes his head in the tipi and shines his flashlight around. If it's gone, then it'll mean he goes right inside the tipi and walks all the way around."

"What'll we do then?"

"Think of something else. But I'm betting he doesn't. Does your great-grandfather have a phone? Can you get in touch with him in the middle of the week?"

"No." Tom was startled by the change of subject.

"Okay. Then you'd better tell him when you see him tomorrow that the ghost dance is definitely on. He can count on having it on Sunday week and that's a promise!"

Chapter Three

The usual Sunday morning battle was fought across the coffee, toast and marmalade. For one awful moment Tom was afraid his mother was going to win and he wouldn't be allowed to go out to the reservation. But then the argument fizzled out, as it always had, and his father bundled him into the car, together with his golf clubs, and they drove off.

— I have to go through with this caper and steal the bundle, thought Tom grimly, digging his hands into the pockets of his down-filled jacket. Not only because of Pete, though that's important. But if I can just find out about myself and let the parents know the way I feel, maybe they'll stop using me for a battlefield. Maybe . . .

"You're very quiet this morning, son. Everything all right?"

"Sure, Dad. Thanks."

"School okay?"

"Sure."

— Only how am I going to explain to Great-grandfather about stealing the bundle? How will he react? Suppose he says I mustn't take it? But he won't do that. After all, it was stolen in the first place, near enough anyway. The white settlers took everything, Great-grandfather's told me that a million times. He should be pleased . . . Why should it be so hard explaining to him how they were planning to rip off one little medicine bundle?

Great-grandfather was standing at the door of his house. Now that it was colder he was wearing an old mackinaw over his buckskins, the bright red plaid jacket outshining the golden poplar and birch leaves.

"Stay for a while, Mark, and enjoy the clean air."

"Sorry I can't, Grandfather. We're teeing off at ten."

In companionable silence the boy and the old chief drank their tea together, and together walked up the hill and through the wood lot to the bluffs above the river. They sat in silence for a while, enjoying the warmth of the sun on their faces, contrasted against the frosty nip of the fall air.

"Something's on your mind, boy," Great-grandfather said after a while.

"If we could get hold of a ghost bundle, Great-grandfather, would you be able to put on the dance?"

"I would. But there are no bundles."

"There are. One anyway." Tom looked sideways at the old chief, at the strong line of jaw and nose and cheekbones, at the arrow-straight glance of his eyes, and quickly make up his mind what to say. "I just heard about it this week. It used to belong to a family called Strathmore, but they died, and I guess . . . well, nobody wanted it. Pete — my friend Pete Cummings — he's really in the know — well, he says he can get it for us."

It sounded a bit weak, but it wasn't an outright lie, not really. Tom looked cautiously at Great-grandfather's face.

The old chief's eyes were filmy with looking into distant times and places. His gnarled hands groped as if he were trying to get hold of something precious. "A bundle? You have truly found a medicine bundle?"

"Yes, Great-grandfather, truly. The ghost bundle. Now will you put on the dance for me?"

The old chief rocked gently to and fro, and sang under his breath in a reedy voice, syllables that Tom had never heard before. "Yes, if I can remember. I must remember. The bundle will help. If it is all there . . . is the bundle whole, unopened?" Tom nodded, and the old man went on. "You must ask your father and mother to be present. And a friend. This Pete . . . will he come if you ask him?"

"Yes, of course. He'd love to. But . . . Mother and Dad? You want *them* to come? I don't think they will." The thought of them being part of the ceremony made him feel awkward, ashamed.

"Nevertheless you will ask them. The friend you must bring. It is necessary. We will prepare a big feast next Sunday and hold the dance as soon as the sun has set. A ghost dance again. . . . !" The old man's face broke into its wonderful warming smile.

Like the sun, thought Tom, and suddenly the whole caper, the danger, the risk of disgracing his father if he should be caught, all this was nothing in comparison to the gift he would be bringing Great-grandfather.

"We must kill a steer for the feast, and boil its

36

tongue for the ceremony." Great-grandfather was thinking out loud. "I must ask Joe Smallbranch to help me. And Amos will build the sweat lodge."

On the way back to the house for lunch he put his arm around Tom's shoulder, a bony arm, feather-light with age. "You and your friend bring me and my people a great gift — our self-respect. I promise you, we will have a ceremony that none of us will forget."

Suddenly Tom noticed that he was almost as tall as the old chief. Either he'd done a lot of growing recently, or the old man had shrunk. Almost a man, Great-grandfather had called him. It made him feel warm with pride, and yet there was a strange sadness in it too.

On Monday he was bursting to talk to Pete, but there wasn't a safe moment until school was finally over.

"Well?" was Pete's greeting.

"Great-grandfather's on top of the world. He's getting ready to hold the dance next Sunday. You're to come too. Is that all right? Will your folks let you?"

"No problem. You mean I actually get to watch the ceremony?"

"I think you're a part of it. Like the best man at a wedding, or a godparent."

"Wow! I'm impressed."

"Just one thing." Tom hesitated and then went on carefully. "I didn't tell Great-grandfather exactly how we were going to get the bundle. I mean, I was scared he'd take it the wrong way and forbid us to go ahead. So I just sort of indicated that it had belonged to this family, the Strathmores, remember? And I said you knew how to get hold of it now nobody wanted it."

Pete nodded understandingly. "That's cool. No problem."

Tom sighed with relief. He hadn't been sure if Pete would think he was just being cowardly. "How did your test with the dollar bill go?" He changed the subject thankfully.

"Perfect. Just the way I predicted. I dropped the bill on the floor behind the exhibit in the tipi, and then I just hung around the gallery until after the closing bell. The guard came to the entrance and told me it was time to leave. He didn't even come into the gallery. Just poked his head around the doorway. Yesterday when I went back the bill was exactly where I'd left it. Our plan's okay, Tom!"

"There's got to be a cleaning staff. I wonder they didn't notice the dollar."

Pete shrugged. "I thought about that. Obviously they don't clean every gallery every day. But it's no problem anyway. The cleaning's not done at night, but in the morning before the museum's open to the public. I went by there bright and early this morning and I saw the janitorial services truck parked at the back."

Tom drew a deep breath. "So there's nothing to stop us now, is there?" His voice sounded a bit shaky and he hoped Pete wouldn't notice.

"Not a thing. Let's plan to go for the bundle Thursday evening." Pete's voice was unnecessarily brisk.

Tom felt a sudden surge of panic. If Pete was

naming days the caper was out of the realm of fantasy. It was real. "Why Thursday?" he hedged. "That's late night shopping. There'll be a lot of people around."

"That's the idea. It's dark by eight. We'll grab the bundle then and mingle with the crowds going home from the stores. The museum closes at six. We'll only have to stay hidden for two hours. The one tricky bit is going to be hanging around near the Indian gallery at closing time, without attracting the attention of any of the guards. We don't want one of them to notice us and then remember he didn't see us leave. Then we'll have to duck into the tipi at the exact moment that the TV camera is looking at the other end of the room."

"It's going to take an awful lot of luck as well as nerve."

"Sure. That's what makes it such fun! And not to worry. If something happens to make it impossible on Thursday, well, we've still got Friday and Saturday to fall back on."

If we have to go through the whole thing twice I don't know how I'll make it, thought Tom, and wished he were more like Pete. Even *talking* about danger put a sparkle into Pete's eyes.

The week tore by, like the week before an exam or a dentist's visit. Tom woke up early on Thursday morning with a sick feeling in the pit of his stomach. For a moment he thought it must be the flu, but then he remembered, and groaned and buried his face in the pillow and tried to crawl back into sleep. But of course it wasn't any good.

He remembered to tell his mother that he'd be having supper with Pete. True anyway, though it wouldn't be at Pete's house, but hamburgers and chips in the museum cafeteria. At school he reminded Pete. "Did you tell your parents you wouldn't be home for supper?"

"Sure. I said there was a meeting of one of the school clubs."

"What club, for crying out loud? There's nothing on yet."

"The Society for the Preservation of Indian Culture," Pete said straight-faced.

"You're kidding! You didn't?"

"Sure I did."

"And they believed you?"

"Certainly. Why not? It's the sort of thing they go in for themselves. Mother said that it was very encouraging that we had activities of that nature in Junior High."

"You're mad, Pete. Totally loopy. Your sense of humour's going to get us into trouble yet."

"See you at five in the cafeteria," was Pete's only response. "Wear a dark jacket and pants, and for goodness sake no squeaky shoes or flashy white runners."

"Master spies aren't the only ones who are trained in this sort of thing," Tom fired back. "I was learning to track through the bush when you were still falling out of your crib!"

Pete was already wolfing down hamburger and chips when Tom arrived at the museum. His face was hot and he looked peculiar, Tom thought, somehow bulkier than usual. "Come on, slowpoke. **Grab a bite.**"

"I'm not that hungry. What's the matter with you? You look as though you were running a fever. Why don't you take off your jacket?"

"Tell you later," Pete hissed between his teeth, and scrubbed his plate clean of ketchup with his last potato chip. "If you're sure you don't want anything let's go and look at those gold things again. It'll fill in the time."

The small upstairs special exhibits room was almost empty this time, and they were able to get a really good look at all the little sculptures, exclaiming how the gold looked as butter yellow and shiny as if the pieces were brand new instead of being hundreds of years old. One of the security guards lounged over to talk to them. "Bet you boys have never seen so much gold in one place in your lives, eh?"

They shook their heads. "It must be worth an absolute fortune," Pete said.

"More than a quarter of a million just for the gold alone, melted down. But the artistic and historical value, well, it's priceless, isn't it?"

"Boy, that's really something! Well, it's ten to six, Tom. We'd better be off and get our homework done."

They clattered down the stairs. The two security guards in the main concourse were talking to a couple of tourists, looking the other way. Tom and Pete ducked quickly into the Blackfoot gallery. It was completely empty, except for the looming figures of the Indian chiefs and braves standing stiffly in their glass cases. One of the chiefs looked a bit like Great-grandfather, thought Tom. His tomahawk was raised and his glass eyes stared in an accusing way.

Pete nudged him. "Let's get out of the way of the TV camera right now. There's a niche beyond that display. Don't stare at the camera. Now! Look, there's masses of room. Nothing but a case with some old bones." He said the words with relish and repeated them. "Old bones. Dry old bones."

"What?" Tom felt a most unexpected shiver run down his spine, and he peered almost reluctantly over Pete's shoulder. Sure enough, curled up in the recessed case, which had been painted to resemble a shallow hole in the ground, was a complete skeleton, the bones dry and powdered with red ochre.

" 'The remains of this Indian woman, found in the course of road building near Rocky Mountain House, are believed to be over a thousand years old'," Pete read. "Wow! Why would they keep a super exhibit like this hidden in a corner!"

Tom stared in fascination. The empty eye sockets stared back at him, and the teeth seemed to be grinning menacingly. A sudden whir of a bell close by made him jump and cry out, the sweat starting on his forehead.

"Sh!" Pete looked cautiously around the corner of the glass case. The gallery was still empty. The camera pointed away from them. "Into the tipi, quick!"

Once they were inside Pete stripped off his jacket, and Tom saw the reason for his unusual bulk. Round his middle were wound several yards of dark brown burlap.

"What on earth?"

"Quick. Climb over the railing and lie down behind the exhibit. Down on the floor as flat as you can."

Tom did as he was told, and Pete flung the length of burlap over him, smoothing out the folds, and then crawled under it himself.

"I got it from the spare room at home," Pete explained. "It's a curtain really, but I noticed that it was almost exactly like the stuff they've got on the floor of the exhibit. Even with a flashlight the guard will never see us. Just additional insurance."

It was hot and dusty under the burlap, even though Tom had to admit it was a super idea, and after a while his nose began to tickle. He pinched it hard and breathed through his mouth until the feeling went away.

Crisp footsteps echoed on the marble floor outside. They came nearer, more muffled on the wooden floor of the gallery. They stopped. Tom couldn't guess how close they were or on which side of the tipi. He felt a sudden wild urge to jump up and shout "Boo!". He dug his nails into the palms of his hands, while the sweat rang down his face. Faintly through the meshes of the burlap he saw a glimmer of light. Then another. He tried to breathe slowly and evenly, but he felt as if his whole body was quivering. The footsteps came again. After a minute there was the ringing echo of shoe leather on marble. Shakily he sat up, cocooned in burlap, and stared at the dim hump that was Pete.

"Whew! That was quite a moment." Pete sat up, his hair ruffled so he looked like a scrawny bird.

"Pete, I nearly jumped up and gave us away. It was weird."

"Me too. This master spy business takes more getting used to than I suspected." Pete held his watch up in front of his face. "Five after six. Nearly two hours to go. We'd better get comfortable under this thing, in case the guard comes back unexpectedly. Only for goodness sake don't go to sleep and start snoring!"

Sleep was the furthest thing from Tom's mind. It wasn't absolutely dark inside the tipi. The big display lights were switched off, but the gallery was still dimly lit, enough to send a triangle of dusty light through the entrance. It fell across the figures of the man and woman crouched by the artificial fire in the centre of the tipi. They were half shape, half shadow. Did the night people look like that, Tom wondered ... if the night people really existed. Only they couldn't really, could they? This was the twentieth century. All that other stuff belonged to the past. Only if it had all gone, perhaps the helping spirits had gone too. Maybe if you believed in one you had to believe in the other. A sort of package deal.

That old woman in the glass case. She'd been dead for a thousand years. Could *her* bones still assemble themselves and walk at nights? Tom suddenly remembered every grisly detail of a tale Great-grandfather had once told him, about a young brave who stopped for shelter one night in a strange tipi, only to wake up in the middle of the night to realise that he was in a death lodge, and that around him the ghostly presences of the dead had reassembled themselves and were sitting in a circle on their bony haunches gambling to the rattle of their own bones.

Tom shut his eyes tight, but that was worse. The folds of burlap were dry and harsh like bony fingers. His eyes jumped open and he stared into the darkness.

"Don't fidget," Pete whispered in his ear.

"What's the time?"

"Twenty after six."

"*Twenty* after! It's got to be later than that, Pete. Your watch must have stopped."

"Uh-huh. Lie still."

Twice they heard the sound of footsteps on the marble floor outside, incredibly loud in the silence that had gone before. Twice they saw the guard's flashlight dimly through the folds of burlap. This night seemed even longer than the nights of vigil he'd spent crouched in the attic, Tom thought desperately. When Pete finally whispered "Okay. Time to go," the words didn't sink in and Pete had to nudge him.

He got stiffly to his feet, while Pete gathered the folds of curtain and wrapped them around him under his jacket.

Pete looked cautiously out of the opening of the tipi. "Wait a moment. The camera's pointing straight at us. Tom, as soon as it's gone I'm going to run to the display case. Be right behind me, and count to forty-five slowly. That's all the time we've

45

got before the camera moves back. Then we'll have to dive for the emergency exit and just rip through, the way we planned. Okay?"

"Yeah." Tom licked his dry lips.

"All right . . . ready . . . Now!"

They scuttled across the room to the shadowy case where the medicine bundles were displayed, and as he began to count Tom could hear the faint scratch of whatever Pete was working with against the lock. A sharp click and the door swung open. Pete's hand shot out and hesitated. "You take it, Tom."

His voice sounded funny, sort of shaky, thought Tom, as he reached in and grabbed the small leather bundle and the card that belonged to it. Hastily Pete pushed the next exhibit over to fill the empty space, and clicked the case shut. "Forty-two . . . forty-three . . ." said Tom aloud.

"Let's go then!"

Together they ran for the wide exit door with the red push-bar and the warning notices. It swung open easily and they tore across the black grass to safety. Pete stumbled on the driveway curb and went headlong into the road. Tom heard the grunt as the breath was pushed out of his body, and turned back.

"You okay?" Tom's heart pounded like a drum. He pulled Pete to his feet and half dragged him through the hedge on to the crescent. Through the thump of his heart and the blood drumming in his ears Tom could hear the alarm bell. The sound seemed to fill the whole night. With it were other sounds, the rattle of bones, the whispery laughter of the night people. Tom caught Pete's arm again and dragged him along the crescent. In one of the houses the lights suddenly went on. Tom felt his muscles quiver, ready to make a bolt for it.

"Steady." Pete's voice was calm. "We're just out for a walk, remember?"

"Are you all right?" Tom asked again.

"Yes, thanks. That was a dumb thing to do. Sorry. I've skinned my knee, but that's about all." He began to brush the leaves off his hair and jacket, and Tom followed suit.

As they turned around the curve of the crescent a figure detached itself from the shadows ahead of them. Tom felt his muscles stiffen. But it was all right. Just a girl and a dog.

"Hi, Marian, fancy meeting you here." Pete's voice was a shade too casual, and Tom realised that this was the little surprise he'd promised. He shot a reproachful look at his friend. If Pete had told his kid sister what they'd been up to . . .

"You remember Marian, don't you, Tom?"

"Sure. Hi."

"Hullo, Tom." Her braces shone in the street light and so did her eyes. She stared up at Tom with such blatant adoration that he found himself blushing. The dog meanwhile, the Cummings's red setter, was jumping up and trying to lick Pete's face.

"Get down, pooch. Guess we'd better be on our way, Tom. Are you coming with us, Marian, or does Rex need more of a walk?"

"Oh, no, he's had plenty." Her voice was breathless with shyness.

47

The sidewalk was too narrow for the four of them to walk abreast, so Tom hustled Pete ahead, leaving Marian and the dog to bring up the rear.

"Why did you have to do that?" he hissed at his friend.

"Sh! Don't worry about it. She doesn't know a thing. I only told her that if she happened to be walking Rex this way she might meet us coming back from the park. She jumped at the chance." There was laughter in Pete's voice.

"Thanks, pal. I'll remember and return the favour some day, you see if I don't. But why? It was a crazy risk to bring her so close to the museum. What if she suspected?"

"Not her. Big brother can do no wrong, while as for you . . . well! It's just insurance, the way I said. Two boys are one thing. They might be up to anything. But two boys, a girl and a large noisy dog, that's something else, don't you agree?"

Tom subsided. Pete was right, as usual. But he still felt uncomfortable with young Marian's worshipping eyes on his back. As they crossed Second Avenue they heard the sound of police sirens to their right. Tom tried to walk on without faltering, as if the sound was unimportant, as it was any other day of the week. They walked on and stopped on the corner of Fifth Avenue.

"Well, Tom, goodnight. I guess we'd better get this hound home before he disturbs the neighbourhood."

"Right. Goodnight, Pete. And, say . . . thanks. I still can't believe it."

"That's all right. It was a blast. And I'm really

looking forward to Sunday."

"See you. 'Bye, Marian. Nice meeting you."

Tom walked home in a dream. It was all over. Things had nearly gone wrong at the last second, but they hadn't. Now, under his jacket, between his sweater and his shirt, was the medicine bundle. The leather felt hard and spiky against his front.

He slipped into the house without being noticed and went quietly up to his room. Carefuly he took out the bundle and laid it on the bed and looked at it.

It was fastened together with a thong of rawhide, and he was tempted to undo the knot and see what was really inside. His hand was right on it when he stopped himself. He wrapped it up in a clean undershirt and hid it behind his socks. Till Sunday, he thought. On Sunday Great-grandfather's hand will be the first to undo the bundle and handle its mysteries.

The mixture of hunger and fear, success and the sudden release of tension had made him lightheaded. He pushed open his bedroom window and looked out. The moon was rising above the roofs, silvering the tops of the trees and the grass. He took a huge gulp of cold night air.

He had a sudden wild longing to strip off all his clothes and go down and dance naked on the lawn. Then he thought of what the neighbours, not to mention Mother and Dad, would say, and in a fit of giggles he went down to the kitchen to fill up on peanut butter sandwiches and milk. It had been a very long day.

Chapter Four

Tom saw with relief that Pete was exactly right with Great-grandfather. He wasn't stiffly on his best behaviour, but he wasn't being too clever either, and he didn't treat Great-grandfather like something out of a Western movie. They took to each other from the first firm handshake.

Great-grandfather served tea, strong and sweet, and Pete supped it with noisy relish. When they were finished they walked up to the bluffs just as if it were any ordinary Sunday, and when they had settled themselves comfortably on the dry yellow grass Tom asked Great-grandfather to explain to Pete why it was so important for young Indians to go in search of their spirits, and to tell him the legends of how the ghost dance began.

"Long long ago in the beginning time," the old chief began, "there was a terrible monster called Wind Sucker that came across the grasslands devouring the Blackfoot people, and they were much afraid. But there was among them a brave young man called Kutoyis, that is, Blood Clot Boy, who had a plan. He went looking for Wind Sucker and allowed the monster to swallow him up, in order that he might kill it.

"Now, once he was inside the monster, and his eyes became accustomed to the dark, Blood Clot Boy saw the skeletons of many people hanging there, and also the bodies of some of his own people who were still alive. So he tied a knife to the top of his head and began to dance, bending his knees and bobbing up and down. And as he danced he sang softly, so that the monster could not hear, 'Oh, you who are still alive and can move, join me in the dance'. And those who were still alive began to bob up and down like Blood Clot Boy.

"Then Blood Clot Boy began to sing louder and louder and his dance became more and more vigorous until he was bobbing up and down right under Wind Sucker's heart, which was hanging in the middle of his stomach. Then suddenly, all at once, he stood straight up, and the knife that he had tied to the top of his head plunged right into Wind Sucker's heart and killed the monster. It fell with a crash that shook the earth, and Blood Clot Boy and his friends crawled out of the dead monster's mouth and went home. Rejoicing, the tribe made a big thanksgiving feast. That was the beginning of the dance."

"But I don't see what that's got to do with the night people," Pete objected.

"That is another story," the old chief said. "And there are many ways of telling it. As many ways as there are people with the memory to hand it down to their children. I had the story from my grandfather when I was a little boy, and this is what my grandfather told me.

"There was once a Blackfoot brave who was separated from his companions after an attack by another tribe. As he was making his way back alone to his own camp he came upon a Blackfoot lodge. Now because it was night and there was no moon he did not realise that what he saw was not an ordinary tipi, but a 'death lodge'. He went quietly in and lay down near the entrance so as not to disturb the other sleepers.

"In the middle of the night he was awakened by the noise of people singing and the sound of rattling bones. He was terrified, because he realised at once what a terrible mistake he had made. He lay very still and he opened his eyes just a slit. Through his eyelids he could see the skeleton feet of many ghosts, all kneeling in a circle, as if they were playing a gambling game. As they sang a little more of them became visible, and after every song the ghosts would try to get to their bony feet.

"Four times they sang and danced, and after the fourth song, during which they were able to stand, the young brave could see every part of their bony bodies except their faces. They sang the four songs four times, and while they were singing for the third time a whole skeleton came into the lodge, brushing past the young brave who had been sleeping near the entrance, so that he felt the touch of its dry bones. This ghost danced by himself and when he had finished he smoked a pipe. Then he turned to the brave and offered him the pipe, and when, trembling, the brave had smoked it and handed it back, the ghost told him to leave and take the ghost dance back to his people. And so he did. And so it was told to my grandfather, who had a ghost bundle, and so my grandfather told it to me."

There was an uneasy silence after the old chief had finished his tale. Even though the sun was still warm and there was no wind Tom found himself giving a great shiver. He remembered the skeleton of the old woman in the museum. I wouldn't go back there now for anything, he swore to himself.

Pete looked at him curiously, and then changed the subject. "Does the rain dance have a story like that, Chief Lightfoot? Can you do it? And does it really work? I don't see how it can. I mean, honestly, if it were going to rain it would anyway whether you danced or not."

The old chief's eyes twinkled. "I do not know if it works, my boy. I have never tried. It is not part of the Blackfoot way. In the south the tribes farmed the land and depended on corn for their survivial, and it was they who began the rain dance: We, the Blackfoot, were never farmers." His voice was scornful. "That was not our way. To us the buffalo was everything, meat and clothes, weapons and tents. For hundreds of years, maybe. I do not know. Then came the white man, far to the south, though our people did not even know of his coming. But the white man fenced the grassland and cut across it with his railway. And he killed the buffalo by the thousand.

"One summer, as it had always been, the buffalo came north, a great brown wave, as far as a man could see to east and south and west. Next year there were not so many, but still enough for the needs of the tribe. The year after that the buffalo came late, and there were very few. By the time they came the Blackfoot people were weak with hunger. They danced and prayed, and when the buffalo finally came there was enough food for the winter, just enough. Enough for clothing and to

53

repair the tents, though not to build any new ones. The year after that there were fewer buffalo still, though the Blackfoot prayed and danced. And then none came." The old chief's story-telling voice was a whisper, as dry as prairie grass, and his eyes dimmed with past-looking. "None. The buffalo was gone for ever. The Blackfoot way was ended."

There was a long silence. After a while Pete asked softly, "What happened then?"

"We lived as best we could." Chief Lightfoot shrugged and then smiled. "We used to burn the grassland all around Fort Edmonton, so that the game would run away. Then the people in the fort could no longer hunt conveniently and they were forced to trade with us, deer meat for good horses and blankets. But more and more people poured out of the east, and now they brought their families, wives and children. It was like a flood. They settled on the land and fenced it round. They would hammer a stake into the ground and call the land theirs. As if a man can own the land we all walk on by putting a stick in it! Such foolishness. but that was the white man's law, it seemed."

"Didn't you fight?"

"Never. There could have been war the time the railway went through our hunting grounds. But Chief Crowfoot said there was to be no more war. He knew in his heart that the buffalo would never come back, and that there was no glory in fighting for a way of life that was already gone for ever. So we signed the treaty and they gave us a little land to farm. But it was hard. We are not farmers. It was never the Blackfoot way."

"There are still some buffalo herds up north. It's a pity they can't develop them again and bring back your way of life."

"Those buffalo are on reservations, same as the Blackfoot. Do you think the buffalo like it up there? When the call to go south stirs in their blood how do you suppose they feel? Do they too remember the great herds, the migrations far to the south in the fall and back again each summer? Do you think perhaps they still remember the grasslands the way they were, open to the sky from the east to west and north to south as far as an eagle's flight?"

Pete nodded. "I guess you mean we can't undo the past, even if it was a mistake. So the only thing left for your people is to change with the times."

"You are right, boy. And yet you are wrong. If we try to live the Blackfoot way as it once was, our people will die out. Yet if each man of us goes his own way in your world, fighting for property, pushing to get ahead, then surely the tribe will also vanish. And what is a people without their tribe?"

There seemed to be nothing more to say. They walked back through the woods in silence. As they helped in the preparations for the dance and the feast, Tom mulled over his great-grandfather's last words. I *am* Blackfoot, he told himself. I won't turn my back on it the way my father did. I won't.

Up on the hill, out of sight of the public road, the men had already built a lodge of skins and boughs, big enough for Chief Lightfoot, Tom and

Pete, Joe Smallbranch and his wife, and Amos Greyfeather and his wife and sons. The rest of the band gathered outside the tipi, ready to listen to the songs and to take part in the feast.

As the red ball of the sun was cut in half by the western horizon Chief Lightfoot led the way to the south of the clearing, carrying the medicine bundle carefully in both hands. He held it high and shouted, "Listen all you dead owners of this bundle, we are going to have a feast. Come and join us. Help us in the dance." Then he turned to the west, the north and the east, and each time he cried out his eerie invitation. Everybody watched silently. Even the dogs didn't bark, and the small children sucked their fingers and stared with huge brown eyes, close to their mothers' skirts.

He entered the tipi, the others following him, going around in a clockwise direction, like the path of the sun. Tom saw that in the centre of the tipi a fire had been made, close to the flat slab of pale stone. Great-grandfather squatted down in front of the stone, facing south, and the others sat too in a circle around the stone. A man Tom did not recognise remained standing in the doorway. Great-grandfather saw Tom's questioning look. "He will guard the entrance against evil spirits," he told them. "While we are busy in the dance and the prayers."

Slowly and carefully Great-grandfather laid the bundle on the slab and undid the stiffened leather thong that held it together. As he flattened out the stiff folds Tom and Pete leaned eagerly forward, but there was not much to see. There were four small leather pokes, like the old-fashioned pouches people once used for tobacco. There was a sheaf of eagle feathers, bent and dishevelled with age, and four small brass bells strung together on a thong. That was all.

Slowly the old chief picked up each object and laid it down again. He opened each pouch and peered inside. He half-muttered, half-chanted under his breath. The others squatted in silence around the fire, and outside too there was a great silence, in which there seemed to Tom to be a striving to help the old man reach back into the past and remember.

'Some grease. I need some beef grease," he said suddenly, and the man standing at the door called over his shoulder to the crowd outside. In a few moments he was handed a cracked cup of beef dripping which was passed up the circle to the chief.

He took some of the grease in his left palm, and mixed with it some powder from one of the small leather pouches. Then with the forefinger of his right hand he carefully painted a large blue circle on the white altar stone. He wiped his hand on the grass and painted a black circle within the blue. Then red, and finally a yellow circle in the centre, like a bull's-eye.

When he had cleaned his hands he took the eagle feathers from the bundle. One he stuck carefully in the ground beside the altar stone and one he fastened upright in his silver hair. Then he handed the others out around the circle. Tom's and Pete's hair was too short for the feathers to stay put, but

Mrs Smallbranch unsmilingly handed each of them a bobby pin.

It should have been hilariously funny, but it wasn't. Tom, glancing round the circle at the shadowy firelit figures, the men in shabby mackinaws, the women in cotton dresses, cardigans and old wool coats, each with a white eagle feather upright in their hair, felt a shiver run through his body that had nothing to do with the evening chill.

Chief Lightfoot took some small boughs of the creeping juniper that grew up on the bluffs, lit them at the fire and laid them on the altar. The juniper snapped and spat as the resin caught, and the sweet pungent smell rose like incense towards the airhole at the top of the tipi. Finally, one by one, the old chief made each person kneel in front of him, while he painted each face with red ochre mixed with grease. He started with Tom and Pete and finished with the sons of Amos Greyfeather.

When all of them had been painted and each was back in his place in the circle around the fire and the altar, Chief Lightfoot picked up the string of bells, and, holding it in both hands, began to sing, moving his hands to and fro and shaking the bells as if he were playing an Indian gambling game. Pete and Tom saw the others imitate the chief, and they too knelt on their heels around the fire with their fists held chest high, moving them from side to side, and then pounding them one on top of the other.

Much of what Great-grandfather sang Tom could not understand, but he heard him pray that

Tom might be strong in the lonely night vigil, and be courageous in facing the attacks of the night people. He asked the ghost owners of the bundle to protect Tom so that no hungry wandering spirit could snatch his mind out of his body while he was waiting for his true spirit to arrive.

After the song and the prayer came a rest, and then another song and prayer, until seven songs and seven prayers had been said. Then the old chief got stiffly to his feet, followed by the others. Again he began to sing, bending his knees and bobbing up and down. Tom remembered the story of Blood Clot Boy, singing and bobbing in the stomach of Wind Sucker until he thrust the knife on top of his head into the heart of the unsuspecting monster. The feathers must represent Blood Clot Boy's knife.

Great-grandfather turned to the west and the songs and the bobbing dance were repeated. Again to the north and then to the east, the others in the lodge copying his movements while he sang.

Then the dance was over and the old chief squatted by the altar, once more facing south. The man who was guarding the door received a birchbark dish from outside and handed it to Chief Lightfoot. It was passed around and each person took a handful of the saskatoon berries it contained. They held out their hands and prayed and then each passed one berry back to the chief, who laid them on the altar. In silence they ate the rest of the berries.

A pot of beef-tongue soup was handed through the doorway, and the chief poured a little into a bowl for each person, and again he prayed and then handed one bowl to the doorkeeper, who took it outside and emptied it onto the ground.

Pete was thrilled. "A libation," he whispered to Tom, his clever eyes sparkling. "Just like ancient Greece." But Tom didn't hear him. He was deeply meshed in the ceremony. As they had danced their bobbing dance it had seemed to him that they were no longer in a tipi, but in the stomach of Wind Sucker, and he felt that the lodge was crowded with many more than the ten people he could see. He remembered the dead bones lying in the museum case, and the long dead owners of the bundle whom Great-grandfather had invited to join them. He felt their presences close around him, suffocating him, and even as the hot soup went down his throat he gave an enormous shudder.

Suddenly everyone else was relaxed, laughing and talking. The men lit cigarettes, and a huge platter of barbecued beef and boiled corn was handed in through the doorway. It was over.

Great-grandfather collected the eagle feathers, laid them with the bells and the bags of coloured powder on the piece of leather, rolled it up carefully and tied the bundle with the thong. He laid it on the altar next to the dead ashes of the juniper.

"Come," he said to Tom, and reluctantly Tom followed him out into the dark night, leaving behind the warm feeling of friendship, the tantalising smell of barbecued beef, and the comforting glow of the fire.

In the clearing around the tipi there were other fires, and there was laughter, and children chasing each other, while the dogs whined and slavered as close to the barbecue pit as they could comfortably get. The smell of roasting meat twisted Tom's stomach and made his mouth water. But Great-grandfather turned away from the lights and festivity and walked up to the edge of the dark wood, where Amos Greyfeather and his sons had built the sweat lodge.

It was small and round, made of bent aspen boughs, rather like an igloo to look at, Tom thought, and it was draped all over with hides and blankets and old coats, whatever could be spared to make a thick insulating cover. As they approached Tom saw men shovelling rocks that had been heated red-hot in a big fire close to the lodge, into a hole in the ground in the centre of the lodge.

"Take off your clothes," Great-grandfather ordered Tom.

"What?" Tom quavered. "Out here?" And as he saw Great-grandfather begin to strip he slowly unzipped his down-filled jacket, shivering as the night air hit his shoulder blades.

"Your clothes symbolize your life, your everyday worries and concerns. They are your wealth, all material things. You must leave all that outside before you enter the sweat lodge." He himself stood naked, bent and skinny, but apparently impervious to the cold, and waited patiently at the door of the sweat lodge as Tom reluctantly shed the rest of his clothes.

"The sweat is very hard, Tom," the old chief

went on. "You must force yourself to be strong so that you can bear it. Remember that what I am able to endure you can endure also. I will not let it get too bad. You must trust me. At the same time you must be humble, remembering that you are as nothing, and that everything there is, the heat of the sun and of the fire, and the strength to endure that heat, all come from the Great Spirit. Remember these things and you will be able to endure the sweat."

The old man got down on his knees and crawled into the sweat lodge. Seeing his skinny buttocks vanishing into the darkness Tom understood that even this low entrance was an exercise in humility. He crawled in after the chief and squatted down opposite him, the pit of red-hot stones between them.

The air was hazy with the smoke of burnt sweet-grass, and the heat of the stones bounced against Tom's face and naked chest. Great-grandfather lifted the ladleful of water from a bucket beside him, poured a little on the ground, sipped some and poured the rest over his head and body.

"Do the same," he told Tom. "And pray for strength." When Tom had drunk and washed, the old man took a handful of sage leaves, gave some to Tom, and began to rub the aromatic herbs over his face and body. Then he called out, "Close the entrance," and at once the men outside began to drape blankets over the doorway.

It was completely dark now, except for the glowing circle of red-hot stones in the centre of the tiny lodge. Tom tried to relax, telling himself that it was really no different from the sauna at the country club. But it wasn't the same, no matter how he tried to kid himself.

From across the red glow of the pit the old chief's voice came, asking for strength from the Great Spirit. There was a mighty hiss as the old man ladled water onto the hot stones. At once the temperature began to climb. The air was filled with scalding steam. Tom felt the sweat pour off his face and arms and chest. He leaned dizzily forward with his head on his knees. The whole world narrowed down to this dark blazing-hot cave-place and the searing heat in his shoulders.

Just when he felt he couldn't possibly hang on for another minute he heard Great-grandfather's voice. "Open the door!" At once the blankets were moved aside. A little wedge of golden light came in from the fire outside, and a wave of pure cold air poured through the small opening.

"Put your head close to the ground and breathe the cool air," Great-grandfather told him, and Tom crouched close to the ground, smelling the frosty earth smells, feeling each separate blade of grass against his naked body.

It felt wonderful, but all too soon the doorway was covered, and once more the heat began to rise, this time to even greater heights. Again, just before it became totally intolerable, the door was opened and the cold air poured in.

For the third time the doorway was closed and the heat rose. Tom felt his head reeling. There was no reality in the world apart from this searing heat. He felt humble and insignificant in the face of it. He lost all track of time. Time seemed to have no meaning.

Then at last the doorway was uncovered again, and Great-grandfather's ceremonial pipe was handed in. He took it carefully, one hand supporting the mouthpiece, the other the carved stone bowl. Tom could see him, half shadow, half lit by orange firelight. He held the pipe above his head. "I am at peace with you, oh Great Spirit, and with my brother," he intoned and then puffed the pipe four times before handing it to Tom.

Tom would have dropped it, his hand was trembling so, only the old man's hand steadied his. "I can't smoke it with you, Great-grandfather," he found himself gasping. "About the bundle — I lied to you."

"Do you want to tell me about it?"

"I must." The words seemed to roll out of Tom as the sweat rolled off his back. He told the whole story of stealing the ghost bundle from the moment when he had first seen it in the museum case. When he had finished he felt very weak, but the searing pain had gone from his shoulders.

"Now you may smoke," was all Great-grandfather said when he finished, and Tom found that he was able to hold up the heavy pipe and pray as the old man had prayed. He handed the pipe back. It was laid carefully aside and the entrance covered with blankets for the fourth time.

"You weren't surprised?" Tom whispered through the darkness.

"No," came the quiet answer. "When I read in the paper that the museum had been broken into, I wondered, though they said that nothing had been taken. And when I saw you I knew."

"At the time it seemed the smart thing to do."

"Do you feel differently about it now?"

"Sure do. I feel awful."

"The sweat has purified you and helped you see things as they truly are." The old man's voice was faint and breathless.

"Great-grandfather, are you all right?" In the old man's weakness Tom felt suddenly stronger.

"Yes." It was less than a whisper.

The heat was more intense now than it had been before. An hour ago Tom would have sworn that it was impossible to endure such heat. Now he felt that he could go on for ever if he must.

"What am I to do?" he asked the old chief humbly.

There was no answer, though he could hear the old man's muttered prayers from across the pit of hot stones. He sank his head to his knees again. It was like being burned at the stake. Like being in the crater of a volcano. Like being in Hell.

He found that the answer was inside himself. "I have to put the bundle back, don't I?"

"You know what you must do."

"Tomorrow. Right after school. Pete will help me again. I'll put it back. I promise."

There was no answer.

"Isn't that enough?" he whispered despairingly. The sweat poured from his body. "What else?" he asked again. "Whatever you tell me to do, Great-grandfather, I will do."

The old man's voice came faintly at last. "It

comes to me that when you return the medicine bundle to its rightful place you will also be searching for your spirit. Thus you will not lose but gain."

"You told me I'd have to look for my spirit alone and in a high place."

"Height is not only how many feet above sea level. It is also in the mind. You can be alone in a crowd and danger can come to you in the middle of the city as well as in the forest or on the moutain. You must put the bundle back alone, and you must tell your friend nothing. Alone and at night you must do it."

"But, Great-grandfather," Tom interrupted desperately. "I won't be able to get into the museum at night."

The old chief went on as if he hadn't heard him. "It must be done at night, for it is only at night that you may find your spirit. Why else did we hold the ghost dance but to protect you from the night people? Listen to my words. You will eat nothing after sunset. You must pray. For four nights you will climb up to the place from which you stole the bundle. If after the fourth night you are not able to put the bundle back in its place you will know that the spirit has refused you. Against that I can do nothing."

"Yes, Great-grandfather." Tom's head sank between his knees.

"Good. The sweat is finished. You are cleansed and ready." Great-grandfather's voice was all at once strong and cheerful.

"Open the door!"

For the last time the blankets were lifted and they crawled out, gleaming with sweat, into the icy night. The fire had died to a glow. The stars overhead were like chips of ice, and to the north, from the horizon almost up to the zenith, the aurora swayed like a green gossamer curtain in the cosmic wind.

A rough towel was thrown over Tom and he was scrubbed and pummelled dry. Then his clothes were handed to him, and in a daze he put them on. How strange his shirt and underpants and socks felt against his skin. He was aware of every nerve-ending and cell in his body, as if he had never really been alive before.

Slowly his great-grandfather and he walked across the grass and down the hill towards the house. There was a car parked outside, just off the road. They walked past the outhouse and the vegetable patch and through the bedroom into the kitchen.

Father was sitting at the table with Pete, while Mrs Greyfeather filled tea mugs. He looked uncomfortable and out of place, and jumped to his feet as soon as he saw Tom and the old man.

"You've kept the boy out late, Grandfather."

"Some things may not be hurried, Grandson. He must have some hot tea before he leaves, to replace all the water he lost in the sweat." Great-grandfather's voice was mildly reproving, and Father subsided, frowning.

"I don't approve of the sweat and practices like that, you know that. It's all superstition," he muttered.

"He is the grandson of my son," was the old chief's only reply.

Tom gulped down a huge mug of sweet strong tea. He hardly had time to finish before Father was on his feet again. As they stood at the door Great-grandfather handed him a bundle wrapped in a piece of old sheet. "Tomorrow night," he said and Tom nodded.

"I promise."

In the car going home he was more than half asleep, and at home he did little more than put the bundle carefully in his bureau drawer before falling into bed. He was almost asleep when he foggily realised if he were to take the bundle back to the museum at night it wouldn't be the relatively simple matter it had been before. If he were to keep his promise to Great-grandfather he'd actually have to break into the museum. There were no two ways about it!

Chapter Five

The cold reality of exactly what he'd promised Great-grandfather hit Tom in the pit of the stomach the instant he woke up on Monday morning. Great-grandfather had made it quite clear, with no room for shilly-shallying. At *night* he was to *climb up* to the museum. That meant instead of walking only eight blocks to Second Avenue and sneaking into the grounds via the bushes that faced the service area, he was going to have to go right down to the river flats, and then climb up the steep bluff of Government Hill, past all the flood-lights . . .

As he choked down his cereal he pictured himself dodging those lights and creeping up on the museum, which was probably being guarded like the Mint since the alarm when he and Pete had taken the ghost bundle. Now the officials would be bound to think that someone was after their precious gold statutes. They'd be on their toes, more than ever. Even if they never saw him getting past the lights he still had to force his way inside through a door or a window. How far could he go before setting off some sort of alarm? . . .

The phone suddenly began to ring and Tom jumped and broke into a sudden sweat, as if it had indeed been the burglar alarm of his imagination.

"For heaven's sake, Tom! What's the matter with you today? You're so jumpy. You nearly had your milk over that time."

"Sorry, Mother."

It was Pete on the phone. "Hey, Tom, be at school early, all right? I want to talk."

"What about?"

"Are you kidding?" Pause . . . "Tom, you will be there, won't you?"

"I suppose so."

"Eight o'clock."

"All right then."

Pete was waiting on the corner by the school, his eyes snapping with curiosity. He started before Tom had even caught up with him. "First off, thanks a lot for having me to the dance and the feast. It was a terrific evening. I wouldn't have missed it for anything. Too bad you weren't there for the barbecue, though. Where did you vanish to anyway? What was going on? I couldn't make head or tail of what Mrs Greyfeather told me."

"Great-grandfather and I took the sweat. It is part of the ritual." Tom spoke reluctantly. Pete was a good friend, the best. In fact, let's face it, he was the only guy he could talk to freely without being laughed at. But sometimes his scientific curiosity got to be too much. An Indian wouldn't have asked personal questions about such matters. He would have known when to be quiet.

"What was it like?" Pete went on eagerly. He didn't seem to notice that anything was wrong. "Why did you have to do that instead of being at the feast?"

"It is hot," Tom explained tersely. "It is for cleansing."

"Like a sauna, eh?"

"Not in the slightest," Tom snapped, and then remembered how he too had compared it with a sauna in the beginning. He smiled reluctantly. "Sorry, Pete. It's just something I don't know how to describe. If I tried I'd just feel stupid."

"Oh, I see," said Pete, in the blank voice of someone who doesn't see in the least. With an obvious effort to change the subject he went on brightly. "Say, I nearly had a fit when Chief Lightfoot gave you the bundle back, right in front of your father, too. I was terrified your father would ask what it was."

Tom grinned. "Not him. He wouldn't want to know. He guessed it had something to do with the ceremony. He won't talk about anything that might be Indian ritual in case Great-grandfather takes him up on it. He's really washed his hands of all that side of his life, you know."

"That's too bad. It's all so interesting. Why did the chief give you back the bundle anyway, Tom? The way he held it at the ceremony I thought he was absolutely thrilled to have it back."

"He was. And when he first heard about it, I thought he was going to cry. But . . . well, you know, you can't fool Great-grandfather, not for long. He knew we'd taken it."

"What! He couldn't have."

"He did. He read about the break-in in the paper."

"But there was nothing at all about the missing medicine bundle. I know there wasn't. I read every line. I don't even think that the museum authorities suspect that it's been taken. Obviously they all

71

think the break-in was an attempt to steal the gold figures. The paper was full of it, descriptions and photographs and everything."

"I know, Pete. I don't understand it myself. Maybe it's ESP or something. But anyway it's the truth. Great-grandfather knew we ripped off the bundle."

"I thought we decided that it wasn't stealing at all? We just repossessed it, remember?"

"Great-grandfather didn't go along with our line of thinking, I'm sure of that."

"Did he actually accuse you of stealing it?"

"He didn't have to. I told him. But he knew already."

"You . . .? Oh, boy! Is he going to tell? No, he'd never do that. Wait a minute. Let me guess. He wants us to put it back again. That's it, isn't it? And that's why you're looking so gloomy this fine day."

"It's something like that."

"Wow, that's some assignment. After our last break-in the museum people will really be on their toes, especially now they've got all that priceless gold on their minds. I suppose Chief Lightfoot wouldn't consider waiting a month or so till the heat's off? . . . No, I didn't think so. Well, not to worry. We'll work on it. Get something really smooth . . ." Pete's eyes sparkled, and Tom's spirits sank still further as he recognised the master-spy expression on Pete's face. Only now he didn't find it so funny.

"Pete . . ."

"You know, Tom, I really think that the

smartest and simplest thing we could do would be just to hang around until the gallery's empty for a moment, and then just leave the bundle on top of one of the display cabinets.''

"Pete . . .''

"Yes, I know, it's unimaginative and its lacks finesse. But with the guards on their toes and touchy the way they're bound to be, honestly I think it's the safest way to go. I'll keep watch at the door while you do it. All you'll have to be careful of is the TV monitor. Just a few seconds and then it'll all be over. It's a pity, and really it's most unjust. Chief Lightfoot should have the bundle. I mean, morally it is his. . . . Anyway the dance was fantastic and taking the bundle in the first place was a jolly interesting experience. Something I've always wanted to try my hand at . . .''

"Pete, will you listen!''

"What's the matter, Tom? Have you got a better idea? Go ahead. I'm listening.''

"I have to put the bundle back by myself.''

"Sure. I'll just hang around the gallery and keep look-out for you.''

"No. All by myself. It's my show.'' Trying to keep faith with Great-grandfather's instructions, Tom found that the words came out much more abruptly than he'd intended.

Pete's face changed. "Oh? Well, if that's the way you feel about it I'm sorry I shoved in. Look, there's the bell. We've got to go anyway.'' He spun on his heel and walked briskly towards the school entrance.

"Pete, I'm sorry . . . I didn't mean . . . I can't . . .''

73

Tom's voice was drowned in the babble and surge of students all fighting to get through the door in the five minutes before the second bell.

All through classes Tom worried about Pete. He was a nice guy all right, but if you rubbed him the wrong way. . . . After school he hung around, but he didn't see Pete and he hesitated to ask anyone else where he was. After all, if Pete was really angry with him, he might have told the others about the ghost dance and the spirit search. They'd get a really big laugh out of that, wouldn't they? Tom Lightfoot, the superstitious Indian, trying to become heap big brave. Would Pete have told? Surely not. But he'd looked awfully mad as he'd walked off. Tom felt suddenly hot and cold all over and sick in the pit of his stomach. He turned his back on the school and ran all the way home.

On Monday nights Mother went out for bridge, and Dad had a political meeting, so supper was very early and there was no hassle over this business of not eating after sunset. His appetite wasn't too good anyway. He pushed his food around and hoped Mother wouldn't notice and start fussing.

After supper there was homework to get through. Maths wasn't bad. The figures were impersonal and behaved themselves like well-drilled soldiers, with no talking back. But social studies was another thing. Give some reasons for the fall of Rome . . . What is an ethical society? These were the sort of questions that set his mind wandering.

Roman gods, superstition, deified Emperor, he

wrote on his scratch pad, and stared at the words. Great-grandfather had poured out an offering to the earth spirits. Was that any different? Was it real while you were doing it and only superstition once it was part of history?

Then that other question ... ethical society. Indian society was a darn sight more ethical than white, if you looked at things like mega-corporations and pollution, and political things like Watergate. But who was running the world? The white people. And who did everyone despise? The red. It didn't make any sense.

Maybe Great-grandfather was wrong. Maybe the only real ethic was to be where everyone else was. Maybe Dad was right all the time and Great-grandfather was hopelessly out of touch, acting out a charade from the past. If Great-grandfather was wrong, then so was the whole idea of seeking out his spirit. And if that didn't make sense, then he really needn't return the bundle either. Only if Great-grandfather was wrong there was no value in the bundle and no reason why he should want to keep it ...

"Thinking's no good," he said aloud and slammed his books shut, after his mind had been round and round in the same track half a dozen times. "The only possible thing is to get it over with."

He put his books away neatly and changed out of his school clothes into a dark roll-neck and jeans. He wouldn't wear his downfilled jacket, he decided. He'd noticed last time how abominably the nylon shell had rustled whenever he wanted to be especially quiet. Instead he slipped on a buckskin jacket that one of his Indian great-aunts had made for him. Mostly it hung in the hall closet. His mother really hated him wearing it, as if it advertised that he was an Indian. For this mission it seemed . . . suitable.

He took the bundle from its hiding place at the back of his bottom drawer and slipped it carefully under his sweater tucking it into the waistband of his pants.

The house was empty. The maid had gone home after doing the dishes. Mother's bridge game wouldn't be over much before eleven, and as for Dad's meeting — he was involved in assisting a fellow lawyer to run for the Liberal party in a local riding — well, it could go on half the night.

For insurance Tom checked that his window was open a crack, drew the curtains carefully across, and then rolled a blanket up under his quilt. With the pillow plumped up and the light off you'd swear he was asleep in bed.

He padded downstairs and let himself out of the house. Nine o'clock. It had been dark for more than two hours. There was a light overcast with neither moon nor stars. He swung off Seventh Avenue and started off downhill towards the river flats. There was nobody else about on foot, though cars zoomed by, their lights picking up the bushes and the median markers and then flashing in his eyes, leaving him blinking, half blinded.

It took him half an hour to reach the river and he quickly began to scramble up the bluffs that rose almost sheer to the bulk of old Government

House, with the museum lying low and modern behind it. It was hard going. It was pitch dark and the ground was hard and the dry grass slippery. Part way up and over to the left was a wooden stairway, but Tom knew instinctively that this climb was in some way symbolic and that to use the staircase wouldn't do. It was like going up the stairs at St. Joseph's shrine in Montreal on one's knees. It was a necessary part of the pilgrimage.

He was out of breath when he heaved himself up on to the lawn that surrounded Government House. He lay still and looked cautiously around. He was in darkness, but the wide circle of grass around the newly restored building was a pool of light. A fly could hardly have made its way across the neatly raked grass without being observed.

For a moment Tom panicked, wishing that Pete were beside him. He swallowed and began to work his way around to the left, moving from bush to bush outside the circle of light, until Government House was behind him and the sprawl of the museum lay ahead and to his right. He lay under a bush to think about it, feeling the cold seep out of the ground into his jean-covered legs.

The front of the museum was hopeless. He could see that right away. The only access in the whole expanse was through the big glass doors that gave onto the foyer and the main concourse beyond. Anyone approaching those glass doors would have to mount a wide flight of stairs and cross an empty paved terrace in full view of whoever was on guard within.

The emergency exits in the east and west walls

were useless as entries. They only opened from within, and anyway, as Tom already knew, they were wired to the central alarm system.

No, thought Tom, biting his lip, the only possible way to break in was to scout around the back of the building, the north side that faced Second Avenue, on the chance that a service door might be unlocked or a window left open a crack. It seemed pretty unlikely, but what else could he do? He didn't have Pete's dubious skill at lock-picking.

Around the side of the museum there was precious little shadow for lurking in, what with the museum floodlights to his right and the street lights to his left and ahead. Feeling naked and vulnerable he made a wild dash for it, and leaned up against the north wall, trying to calm his breathing and the wild beating of his heart. I'd make a rotten criminal, he thought ruefully, and then ... I *am* a criminal. At least if I succeed ... Breaking and Entering ...

Slowly he worked his way along the whole of the north wall. He found no openable windows, but there were eight doors, including two fourteen foot high ones that must be used for trucks loading and unloading exhibits. He tested each door as he came to it, half of him wanting it to open, the other half praying that it would be locked. When he'd made the whole tour of the north side he sequeezed through the bushes on to Second Avenue and slouched off home, feeling cold and foolish, and unaccountably angry with Great-grandfather.

To cap an unsatisfactory evening there was a

light on in the study window. Dad's meeting must have wound up early. So he was forced to sneak around the back of the house and climb up the trellis on to the sunporch roof, and get into his bedroom through the window.

Next morning Pete greeted him with a grin, as though nothing had gone wrong between them. "You get the bundle put back okay?"

Tom shook his head and scuffed at the leaves remaining in the gutter.

"Why not?"

Tom shrugged. "It was locked up tight. I couldn't get in. I really tried."

"Oh, for crying out loud! You mean you tried to put it back at *night*, after the place was closed? Why didn't you do it the way I said? Good grief, that place must be like a fortress, guarded, burglar-alarmed . . . how did you expect to get in?"

"I thought maybe I'd get lucky . . . a door unlocked, something."

"Why don't you stop being obstinate and leave the thing in the gallery during viewing hours?"

"I can't. It's no good."

"Oh, for Pete's sake, Tom! Just because I suggested it . . ."

"It's not like that, honestly."

"Then it's the old chief. That's it, isn't it? It's some crazy idea of Chief Lightfoot's. Ah-hah! You should see your face. That's it, all right."

"He's not crazy. He didn't get to be chief by being crazy. He's not just hereditary chief, you know. The band elected him as well, and that doesn't often happen.

"Sorry, sorry. But I got the impression that you were kind of fed up with the old man."

"Maybe. But I won't stand for other people calling him names."

"All right. Forget I said it. Tom, why won't you let me help you? It'll be much harder but I bet I'll be able to find a way of getting in, even at night."

"No! Thanks, Pete, but no."

"Okay, fellow, if that's the way you want it. You can't say I didn't try to help you out." There was a funny expression on Pete's face. He shrugged and walked off, and Tom had a hollow feeling in his stomach that he'd just lost something important. And he didn't have so many friends that he could afford to throw one away.

He tried to imagine how Pete must be feeling, being invited to share in something really special and private, like the ghost dance, and then the very next day being rejected. I'd be as mad as fire too, thought Tom. If only Great-grandfather hadn't said that I mustn't tell him . . .

Suppose now he is angry enough to tell the other guys? He might. I wouldn't really blame him. I'd die if they found out about the ghost dance and the spirit search. I'd have to quit school. That's what I'd do. I'd quit school and go and live on the reservation with Great-grandfather.

In Social Studies there was a discussion on superstition. Tom slouched in his desk and tried to be invisible. Some of the things people said . . . it was just as if they knew. He glared accusingly at Pete, but Pete didn't see him, or wouldn't see him. I hate him, thought Tom. I'd like to kill him.

After school Pete and some of the others played touch football. Tom wasn't even asked. He walked slowly home, scuffing up piles of golden poplar leaves and kicking them across the sidewalk. "You can be alone in a crowd," Great-grandfather had said, and the memory of the bitter heat of the sweat came back to him. "All right," he told himself grimly. "If this has got to be part of it, okay."

He got most of his homework done before supper, and then lay down on his bed for a short nap. He woke with a start to find that it was already dark outside. He jumped up . . . supper . . . and nearly fell over a tray lying on the floor outside his door. There was a can of pop, two huge peanut butter sandwiches and an apple.

How come, he wondered, as he picked up the tray, that Mother can be so super thoughtful about some things, and yet about others, like trying to understand Great-grandfather and the Indian way of life, be so rotten? He'd never understand people, never. Except for Great-grandfather. He was the only person who was clear all the way through.

He looked at his watch. Nine o'clock! He'd been asleep for more than three hours. His stomach growled and knotted at the sight and smell of the peanut butter sandwich, but he resolutely pushed the tray aside and made his preparations. He'd eat when he came back, when it was all over. He must go fasting, or it wouldn't work. Great-grandfather had said so.

He couldn't tell if anyone was home. The house was quiet. All he could hear was the ticking of the clock in the hall, but Dad could well be dozing over the paper in his study, with a clear view of the stairs. To be on the safe side he went through the window.

It was a dreary repetition of the night before, the long walk down to the river, the crawl up the hill, the dodging from bush to bush in constant fear of being seen, the testing of each door, the feeling of fear that a door might indeed open under his hand, the despair when it didn't.

It's hopeless, he thought. I'm an idiot even to go through the motions. Two more nights to go, and they'll be just as hopeless. He had just crawled through the bushes on to Second Avenue when a shadow detached itself from the deeper shadows of the shrubs.

"Hi." The voice was quiet and friendly, but Tom's skin tightened all over and his heart gave a violent thump. He tensed himself to make a run for it, and then looked again.

"*Pete?*"

"Who else."

"What in *hell* are you doing here?" Tom pulled him by the arm until they were on the sidewalk and walking away from the museum grounds.

"I just dropped by to see how you were doing. I phoned you earlier but your mother said you were sleeping. Then I phoned half an hour ago and there was no answer. So I figured you had to be here. I wanted to talk."

"I don't know what about. You've done all the talking that's necessary, don't you think?"

"What's that supposed to mean?"

"You had to go and blab to the other guys about the ghost dance and everything, didn't you?"

"What makes you think I'd do a thing like that." Pete stopped suddenly under a street light. In the bluish glare his face looked pale and furious.

"I saw how the guys looked at me in social studies. It was a rotten thing to do, Peter Cummings."

"Boy are you ever paranoid," Pete shouted. "I never told them a thing. It's all in your mind, stupid."

"Stupid yourself," Tom replied automatically, and then stared. "You mean, you really didn't say anything . . . to anyone?"

"No I didn't. And thanks for the vote of confidence. Now I'll tell *you* something. I'm fed up with you, Tom Lightfoot. You can't go and let a person be part of something important, like the ghost dance thing, and then suddenly slam the door in their face, and not let them help or be part of things or anything."

"I can't. I *told* you that."

"Without me you'd never have got the bundle in the first place, and then your great-grandfather wouldn't have been able to hold the dance. Without my help you're never going to be able to put the thing back again either, not if you're going to do it in this cock-a-mamy way in the middle of the night."

"I'm sorry," Tom stammered.

"It's that dumb pride of yours. I bet I could unlock one of those doors for you. You want me to try? We could go back right now. I can do it, I bet.

You've only got to ask."

"No! Heck, Pete, I've told you I've got to do it alone."

"Okay, then, fellow. Lotsa luck!" Pete turned away.

Tom swallowed. "We can at least walk home together, can't we?" Pete was right about his pride, he thought ruefully. That request really stuck in his throat. If Pete turned his back on him now that really would be the end of a good friendship.

Maybe Pete realised it too. Anyway he gave a reluctant grin and shrugged his shoulders carelessly. "No law against it, I guess. The sidewalk's free."

Chapter Six

Wednesday was Hallowe'en and there was a dance at school in the afternoon. Tom had the odd feeling of being in two worlds at the same time. One moment he was in the school gym dancing to the beat of the rock band on record, the next he was in a fire-lit tipi, with an eagle feather in his hair, bobbing up and down like Blood Clot Boy to the rhythm of Great-grandfather's chant.

He was in the same dream state all afternoon, and he didn't even notice that Mother had his favourite lamb chops for supper. Homework was an unbearable drag, and by the time he was free to leave for the museum he had begun to loathe the whole adventure.

Why am I *doing* this? he asked himself, as he pulled on his roll-neck and dark jeans. I'm so tired. It's hopeless anyway. Maybe it would be easier to give up the whole idea. Just *do* what Father wants and become a white lawyer. It'd make Mother happy too. Play golf on Sundays. Lock into the system. Why not? Most people do, don't they? I'd probably be happy enough once I got used to it . . . But even as the thoughts went through his head he knew he was only kidding himself.

The weather had changed, he found as soon as he'd left the house. Indian summer was over and winter was around the corner. There was frost riming the dead leaves on the sidewalk, and ice gleamed darkly in patches on the road. Once he had left the tree-lined residential streets he could see the stars blazing white and hard in the black sky. He shivered and pushed his hands deep into his pockets as he jogged down the road towards the river.

He was later than usual. It was well after ten. As well as doing his homework he'd had to answer the door and hand out Hallowe'en goodies to the neighbourhood trick-or-treaters. Then Mother had trapped him into helping her search for some bridge tables which should have been in the basement storage room, but weren't. It was almost ten before he'd run them to earth up on the rafters of the garage.

"I have to have them for tomorrow afternoon," Mother had said. "Just get the worst of the dust and cobwebs off outside, dear, before you bring them in. I'll have Gertrude clean them properly when she comes tomorrow."

Bridge parties, he thought with disgust, and wondered what sort of woman *he'd* eventually marry. Someone to walk through the woods with, he thought vaguely, and not talk unless he felt like talking too.

Patches of ice were sailing down the river from the high country, looking like a pale Armada on the dark stream. His hands froze climbing the bluff, and his breath was coming in painful foggy puffs by the time he reached the top.

It was all so familiar now it should be a cinch, he told himself. He'd scouted the building for two nights now. He knew every bush and every patch of useful shadow. Old hat ... So why did his stomach feel so churny? And his skin crawl with nerves? It was as if part of him knew that he was pressing his luck. Twice lucky. The third time . . .? That's how it felt.

Sliding from shadow to shadow, willing himself to be invisible in the lighted areas in between, he skirted around to the back of the museum and began to try the doors. It was almost a mechanical thing by now. And he knew full well that they'd be locked. They always had been. It was only for Great-grandfather. Turn the knob. Push. Quietly release. On to the next door. Turn . . . push . . . release . . . quietly now. No click of the latch to give him away to the guard who might possibly be lurking on the other side. Turn . . . push . . .

When the fifth door gave way it was so unexpected that he nearly fell over as it swung open with his weight on the knob. The noise he made was probably small enough, but it sounded disastrous in the echoing space in which he found himself.

He stood, heart pounding, his hand frozen on the door knob, waiting for the jangle of the alarm system that he had imagined so often in his restless dreams. But there was nothing. The silence was total. It was like being in a tomb. When he let out his breath at last in a ragged sigh it sounded unbelievably loud.

Slowly he closed the door behind him, and for the first time realised the oddity of something else. He was in total darkness, a blackness as complete as the silence. Somehow he'd taken it for granted that the back quarters of the museum would also be lit. He must have come into some sort of passageway with store rooms or offices off it. He just had to feel his way along and he would come to the lighted area.

Then he stopped and frowned. Why had the door been unlocked in the first place? It was really an incredible coincidence. Was it a trap? Maybe in a moment the lights would glare on, leaving him blinded and defenseless, and he would hear the guard's voice ... "Halt or I shoot! ..." Did security guards carry guns? He couldn't remember. He licked his dry lips and stood hesitating in the darkness and the silence.

If only Pete were beside him, backing him up. Thinking of Pete he remembered. "I bet I could unlock one of those doors for you. Want me to try?" Pete had said, and he'd said "No", and Pete had walked home in a temper. Only not for long. Good old Pete. Tom smiled with relief. It was okay. He hadn't asked Pete for help, but Pete had come along on his own to lend a helping hand, unlocking a door on the quiet. Everything was all right. He'd obeyed Great-grandfather, and kept his part of the bargain ... he hadn't *asked* for help. It had been given. Only where was Pete now? Lurking outside to lend another hand if needed? Or maybe he'd just unlocked the door and gone home chuckling at the thought of Tom's surprise. That was like Pete. Just like him.

Tom felt a comfortable warmth and a new surge of confidence. Now if he'd only got the little flashlight in the pocket of his buckskins everything would be great. Anxiously he dug in. Pocket knife. Compass. All the paraphernalia of camping. Yes, there it was. Only a penlight, but the battery should be good for a few hours yet. He'd put it in just before his last camping trip.

He pushed the button and the thin beam of light shot out. It looked a bit anaemic in here. He flashed it around. He was in a huge place, not a corridor at all, but something more the size of a small aircraft hangar, packed with tables and boxlike shapes and strange shadowy lumps.

There was a most peculiar smell in the air. He identified paint, something like mothballs, something else chemical, and a furry animal smell like the zoo on a warm day. The tiny beam of light caught the shadow of a naked tree, a rock, a glimpse, unbelievably, of blue sky. What on earth had he fallen into?

The beam was too small to reach the far side of the room, so, swallowing a sudden lump in his throat, Tom began to move cautiously to his right, looking for some sort of way out to the front part of the museum. He felt along the wall, skirting obtacles carefully, always in terror that he would make some sudden noise that might bring a guard running. Each time he came to a door he switched off the flashlight, quietly eased open the door and listened, before switching on the light again. Each time the door opened only onto darkness.

The first door led to a small store room, neatly stacked with cardboard boxes. Closing it softly he moved on, conscious all the time of the minutes ticking by, of the possibility that in any one of these minutes a guard might suddenly enter, throw a light switch and catch him standing there. 'Breaking and Entering' The phrase jumped unbidden to his mind. He imagined Dad's face if he should be arrested. He swallowed and cautiously eased open the second door. Another storage area. Paint cans and big barrels of chemical stuff this time.

Flashing the inadequate light this way and that he picked his way past a couple of trestles and a worktable. Something large, dark and shapeless loomed up directly in front of him. There was a momentary flash. He stared. Were his eyes starting to play tricks on him? He moved the flashlight slowly. No mistake, it was there again. The baleful glare of two eyes staring unblinkingly at him from no more than ten feet away.

Tom backed up so fast that he knocked over one of the trestles. It slid and clattered to the cement floor with enough noise to waken the dead. He froze and held his breath. Would the guards have heard that? Surely they must?

The eyes never blinked. Were they coming closer, or was it his imagination? He looked over his shoulder. The exit wasn't far behind him. He'd only to turn and slip through it, and he would be out of this horrendous place for ever. If he walked home fast he'd be in his room before his parents even returned. Nobody would know he'd run away from his vigil. Nobody need even know that he'd found an open door. After all, a guard could easily have found it and relocked it after Pete had done his fancy jimmying tricks . . .

Then the old chief's voice came to him, not his ordinary everyday voice, but the faint sing-song story-telling voice. "He might become afraid of the night people, the ghosts of the dead, and run back to the tents of his family — still a boy, unguided and purposeless."

"All right, Great-grandfather," said Tom under his breath, and gritting his teeth and holding the flashlight stiffly in front of him like a weapon, he walked forward until he was face to face with the lumpish shadow. The twin lights gleamed redly back no more than two yards ahead of him. A yard. Still they never moved, and there was no noise in the room except for the sound of his own breathing.

Cautiously Tom stretched out a hand and touched fur. He snatched his hand back as if it had been burned and caught his breath in a gulp of fear. But still the thing never moved. He swallowed and came right up to it, and suddenly the oddness of the whole room fell into perspective and he nearly laughed out loud with the sheer relief of it.

He was standing nose to nose with a stuffed bison. The whole room was filled with a muddle of worktables, half stuffed birds and animals, painted panoramas, and dioramas complete with sky, real trees, rocks and grass. He was in the workroom of the big Habitat Natural History gallery.

Tom leaned his head against the shoulder of the great beast. Oh, you buffalo, you, he said to himself. You nearly made me the greatest idiot of the century. Running away from a stuffed buffalo! That was a joke for a boy who aspired to be a Blackfoot brave.

He leaned against the shaggy hair and tried to imagine what it must have been like in the old days, waiting for the herds to come north out of a cloud of dust and the sound of thunder. Imagine stopping a charging buffalo with an arrow, or herding the whole earth-shaking, dust-raising mass over a buffalo jump with nothing but waving arms and shouts. And he, Tom Lightfoot, descendant of those braves, had been spooked by one tired old stuffed fellow in a museum workshop.

Still chuckling to himself he tiptoed along the wall, keeping his flashlight low. He didn't want to trip over any more trestles . . . he'd been lucky so far. The last door on his right wouldn't budge, but when he ran the flashlight beam up the jamb he saw that it was secured only by a simple bolt near the top. He slid it back smoothly and switched off his flashlight, in case its beam might alert a guard somewhere on the other side.

It felt bigger, this time, not like a closet. Maybe he'd struck it lucky at last. Only there was an awful smell. Acrid. Rotten. It made Tom gag and breathe shallowly though his mouth. There was a noise in there too, the first sound he'd heard since he'd come through the outside door. It wasn't a human sound, he was sure of that. But it certainly didn't sound mechanical either. It was a very faint continuous rustling, munching, slithering, clicking kind of noise.

Almost he stepped back and shut the door without turning on his flashlight at all. Then, "Ancestors, help me," he whispered, remembering Great-grandfather's prayers during the ghost dance, and with a reluctant sense of something too awful to be looked at, he switched on the light.

He must have stared for about ten seconds, his brain not able to take in what his eyes saw. Then, his hair bristling on the back of his neck, he let out a horrendous yell and backed out of the room, slamming the door.

The sound echoed through the room. The flashlight slipped out of his suddenly sweaty hand and rolled, still lit, under a bench. He dived after it as if his life depended on it. Thank goodness nothing had broken and it still worked. With shaking hands he jammed back the door bolt as if the things inside could really come out after him.

"Oh, no. Oh, Great-grandfather, I can't . . ." he moaned, and then suddenly shivered all over as a stray piece of sacking tickled the back of his hand. Wildly he began to brush himself all over and search around with the flashlight. Then he sighed and dragged a hand over his sweating face. He put his hands over his eyes as if he could physically push away the memory of what he'd seen. What *was* this place? Was he mad, or dreaming? Had the Night People snatched his mind, and was that what it was like? Were all Great-grandfather's tales of the spirit world really true after all?

After a few minutes shaking Tom managed to calm himself down. "I'm in a city in the middle of the twentieth century," he told himself firmly.

"This is only a museum. Whatever it was I saw has got to have some perfectly reasonable scientific explanation."

Only what had he really seen? He swallowed and deliberately made himself remember. It had seemed to be a huge glass case, like a giant aquarium, but filling almost the whole room. Inside it had been the skinned and gutted carcass of a large animal — a wapiti maybe, or a moose. Nasty and unexpected, but nothing more.

It was the other things. He shivered. The whole carcass had been *alive* — no, not really alive, though for a minute he'd been fooled. He shuddered again and tried to think scientifically, the way Pete would. The carcass had been *covered* — that was it — covered with thousands and thousands of small beetles munching and tearing their way down to gleaming bone.

He swallowed again and hoped that he wasn't going to be sick. Nervously he swung the flashlight around the edges of the door. Suppose some of those heaving thousands should find their way out? There was a large sign on the door. Too bad he hadn't noticed it sooner. It said baldly:

BEETLE ROOM
Keep locked at all times

"You bet," Tom said feebly to himself. "By all means keep locked. Always." He turned away and moved to the end wall of the workroom. His hand hesitated on the knob of the next door. What else might he find in this Chamber of Horrors?

Well, he couldn't stay here all night. He opened the door cautiously and listened. Nothing. He turned on his flashlight. It reflected nothing but the small moonshape of itself off a burlap-covered wall. The air smelled different. Fresher. More ordinary. He flashed the light to right and left. A corridor, quiet and empty.

Thankfully he slipped out of the big workroom and turned to the right. There was no particular reason. It just felt lucky. After about twenty feet the corridor turned left. Now there was carpet underfoot. To his left there was the gleam of glass, reflecting himself, a pale ghost. Way ahead of him there was a faint glow, not really a light, but a slight lessening of the solid dark.

His feet silent on the carpet, Tom moved along, his right hand against the wall, his left holding the now switched-off flashlight. He must be very close to the main concourse. Slowly, he told himself. Go slowly. Suddenly his right hand felt space instead of wall. To his right the carpet was replaced by marble. He could feel its cold slipperiness. There was a sensation of immense openness.

It looked completely different at night, but after a few seconds he realised that he was standing at the east end of the concourse that separated the two wings of the museum. There was faint starlight coming through the glass that overlooked the courtyard to his right, and he thought the moon must have risen. He could see faint indistinct shadows under the planters and benches out there.

When he moved quietly forward, his feet cautious on the echoing marble, he became aware

of a light source other than the moon and stars —
the array of floodlights on the terrace outside the
main entrance over to his left. He stared. Why
should they still be on and the interior of the
building be in darkness? Something was wrong.
Why hadn't the alarm sounded when he'd pushed
open the outside door? Pete was crafty all right,
but surely he wasn't *that* crafty? The trouble was
with all his talk about master spies you were never
sure when he was kidding and when he wasn't.

Tom waited for a moment, leaning against the
wall that separated the wide two-storey concourse
where he stood from the front reception area.
During the day one or two security guards were
always there. Surely at night you could expect to
find at least one? And why would he be sitting in
the dark as if nothing was wrong? None of it made
any sense.

He frowned, remembering the noise he'd made
in the workroom. Why hadn't that brought out the
guards? What were they all doing? Waiting to grab
him red-handed? Was the whole museum a trap?

Uneasily he peered round the corner. As far as he
could see in the light cast by the floodlights
outside there was no one in the front area at all. It
was all most peculiar, but at least the darkness was
his ally. The unlocked door through which he had
come had brought him out from the back regions
to a spot exactly opposite where he wanted to be.
To reach the Blackfoot gallery he would have to
cross the open marble floor in full view of the front
area, both galleries, the stairs and the balcony of
the upstairs lounge. He wondered how much of a

silhouette he would make in the faint light coming from the courtyard to his right, and he looked around for an alternative route.

But in the end he decided that the quickest and simplest way was the best. He slipped off his runners and tied the laces together through one of the belt loops of his jeans. Then, his socked toes slipping on the marble, he sprinted across the width of the concourse and didn't stop until he'd gained the shadows that engulfed the entrance to the Blackfoot gallery.

Flat against the wall he fought to control his breathing and the pounding of his heart was so loud in his ears that it drowned out any other sound. He waited and listened. In frozen silence the museum waited back. He tiptoed into the dark gallery, instinctively looking up to where he remembered that the TV camera was installed. Then he almost laughed out loud. If *he* couldn't see a hand in front of his face, it was reasonable to assume that the camera couldn't either.

The idea brought him up short again. What *were* the guards doing ... sitting in the dark, looking at a series of blank monitors? There seemed to be no rational answer, so he pushed the thought to the back of his mind, and, moving cautiously, one foot at a time, his arms outstretched, he walked into the dark and windowless gallery. If he could find his way without risking the flashlight for the TV camera to pick up, so much the better.

He had to go to the right, he remembered, past the chiefs and braves in their beaded regalia.

You're only wax, he told them firmly, as he tiptoed past in his socked feet, the memory of their black eyes burning his back. Now he should be close to the open part of the gallery where the replica of the tipi stood. If he stuck to the left hand wall he should come level with the case where the medicine bundles were displayed in about ten strides.

He found it easily, even in the dark. It would have been perfect if he could have jimmied open the cabinet and put the bundle back exactly where he'd found it, but Tom knew he couldn't begin to match Pete's lock-picking skill, especially in the dark. He'd please nobody if he made a mistake and broke the glass. Thankfully he took the ghost bundle from its hiding place between his sweater and skin and laid it carefully on top of the cabinet.

There. It was like a huge weight rolling off his shoulders. Now nobody would ever know who had taken the bundle or why. He had done exactly as Great-grandfather had bidden him, he'd fulfilled his spirit quest within the allotted four days and still got away without endangering Dad's chances of being appointed judge.

With a heady sense of relief he turned to retrace his steps, his right hand lightly guiding him along the wall, the switched-off flashlight in his left hand. Just past the tipi was the emergency exit. Then home . . .

He'd only taken four steps when his trailing foot caught on something lying on the floor, and he sprawled full length with a crash enough to waken the dead.

Dead. Why'd he thought that? It was a perfectly

stupid phrase. There were no dead here to waken. Then, in sudden memory of the dry red-ochred bones of the old Indian woman, he began to hunt frantically for the flashlight that had shot from his outstretched hand as he had fallen. It was stupid to start thinking about bones. He'd better start thinking about what he'd say to the security guard who was bound to come charging into the gallery at any moment, after all the noise he'd just made.

Over to the left, surely. Oh, where was that flashlight? He couldn't leave without it — fingerprints and all. He shuffled forward on his knees patting the floor with his hands. Damn! Could it have rolled this far? Or had he somehow got turned around in the dark?

His fingers touched something cold and metallic, and he sighed with relief. But almost before the breath was out he felt the skin crawl at the nape of his neck. It was a flashlight all right, but it wasn't *his* flashlight. This one was large, a searchlight practically. He pushed the button up and down, but nothing happened, and a second later his fingers told him why. The lens and the bulb were shattered.

Whose flashlight? And why should it have been left in the middle of the floor? And what had he tripped over? It couldn't have been the light. It was something much heavier, much bulkier.

Reluctantly his hand went out again, just beyond where he'd picked up the light. His fingers touched a hand. He managed to bite back the yell that rose in his throat, but the groan that came out instead was loud enough to hear, if there had been anybody around to hear.

The hand was limp, as if it didn't belong to anybody, and it felt horribly clammy. Unwillingly Tom made his hand explore up the arm, across the shoulder, the back of the head.

The man was lying on his face. His clothes felt like uniform. His hair was short and thin on top. Somehow that felt worse than anything, that bare scalp. It made the man seem even more vulnerable, like a baby.

Tom tried to find the carotid artery at the side of the man's neck, the way he'd seen it done on police shows, but his nerves were jumping and his heart pounding so much that he couldn't be sure if he could feel a pulse there or not. His fingers touched the back of the man's neck and came away sticky wet. He found himself staring at his hand in the darkness and then rubbing it frantically against the back of the man's jacket.

If only Pete were here. He'd know exactly what to do. He'd have a flashlight. He probably knew first aid. Anyway he'd have a plan. What had happened to the guard? Maybe it was a heart attack. That must be it. He'd fallen and hit his head against one of the display cases as he fell . . .

Hit the *back* of his head? Sure, it could have happened that way, he told himself. If the man had fallen backwards that's exactly how it would have been. Only why was he lying sprawled on his *front* in the middle of the gallery away from the display cases?

It was more as if the man had been investigating something and had been slugged from behind.

Only what had he been looking for? It couldn't have been Tom. He must have been lying on the floor for ages before he himself got there and fell over him.

He remembered the flashlight in the man's hand. Of course, the lights had gone out and all the guards had gone round investigating. And then in the dark someone had slugged him. Only who? And why? And the other guards . . . what had happened to them?

Unthinkingly Tom rubbed his hand across his face, and felt his fingers still sticky. He shuddered. Then the truth came to him in a blinding flash, and he forgot about the blood of the guard and the bones of the old woman, and everything except the fact that someone else had broken into the museum tonight. Someone else had jimmied open a door slugged the guards and stolen the gold figurines from Mexico. It hadn't been Pete who had opened the door. It had been *them*. And it was *they* who had cut off the lights and the alarm system.

And he was stuck slap in the middle of it all. Sooner or later a passing police car would notice the darkened museum and investigate. They'd find the gold was gone. They'd find the unconscious guard. And if he didn't hurry up and get out they'd find *him*, with the guard's blood all over his hands. Oh, *where* was that flashlight!

Frantically he felt the floor around the guard's body. There it was, rolled right up against the man's leg. Please, God, don't let it be broken.

He switched it on. The man looked awful. The

hair at the back of his head was wetly dark and a little trickle ran down behind his ear. His face, what Tom could see of it, was a horrible clay colour.

Still crouched by the body Tom swung his flashlight round. The emergency exit was right across the room from him. He could bust right through and be away from this mess and home in fifteen minutes. This time the alarm wouldn't even go off. He'd be free and clear. It was so simple.

Only it didn't take into account the injured guard. How bad was he? As Tom hesitated, on one knee beside the man, he became aware of a sound. How long had it been going on? It was a tapping sound, a regular faint persistent tapping, and it seemed, in the face of all scientific possibility, to be coming from the case in the niche, the one which contained the bones of the old Indian woman.

Wildly Tom waved his flashlight around the gallery. The TV camera didn't matter any more. Where was the tapping coming from? There was nothing to see, and nothing moved but the shadows and the reflection of his flashlight in the glass cases. Like cats' eyes in the dark, he thought, and remembered the stuffed bison in the workroom.

"I am not afraid of you, oh you Night People," he muttered under his breath. "I am protected. You cannot hurt me."

Still the tapping persisted. He forced himself to his feet and stiffly faced the source of the sound. He played the flashlight over the display case, biting his lips.

What did he really expect to see? Did he really think that, as in the story of the man in the death lodge, the bones might indeed have come to life, that they would be kneeling in the case, swaying rhythmically to and fro, while the clenched knuckles tapped bonily against the glass as they shook in the gambling game? After all, it was Hallowe'en night.

The sweat was running into Tom's eyes and he was gasping as if he'd just swum four lengths. Holding the flashlight steady he wiped the arm of his jacket across his face, and blinked his eyes.

The bones lay dustily in their eternal sleep. The tapping, he realised, once the waves of fear had subsided, was coming from *behind* the case. Only there was nothing there but the bare wall, and a heating pipe that ran from the floor up to the upstairs gallery.

Now that his ears weren't thundering with his own irrational fear he could hear the signal quite clearly. Any kid would have recognised it, whether he knew Morse or not. It was the universal plea for help. Three shorts, three longs, three shorts S . . . O . . . S. Over and over again, tapped out on the hot water pipe in the gallery upstairs, the gallery next to the room where the gold figures were displayed.

Chapter Seven

Afterwards, when the whole story was straight in his mind, Tom reckoned that he couldn't have hesitated for more than a minute at the most, but at the time it seemed to be forever, while the alternatives flowed through his mind and the action slowed down to the dream speed of a shampoo commercial.

The emergency door was right in front of him, no more than twenty feet away. He could get out of the museum before 'they' caught him, if 'they' were still here, or before the police arrived and arrested him. After all, a shrewd clear voice in his mind argued, the most important thing was to keep his family name out of the paper and the police court. He could always stop at the nearest phone booth and warn the police, if they hadn't found out already, that the museum had been broken into and one of the guards injured. That would be good citizenship. That would be the intelligent move. That's probably what Pete would advise him to do.

But another part of him, a more slow-thinking inarticulate part, told Tom that there was really no choice at all, that the only possible thing for him to do was to go upstairs in response to the SOS.

The shrewd voice argued that there was no point in doing that.

— Maybe the thieves are still up there. You could get hurt too, and that wouldn't help anyone.

Better to get out now and find a telephone.

— But they could kill the guard while you're running around looking for a phone booth.

— They could kill you too, Tom, if they were to catch you.

— Maybe. I've got to risk that.

— Don't be so selfish. You're not running away for your own sake, you know. It's for Dad. You wouldn't want to risk him losing a chance of that appointment.

— Of course not. But I've got to help.

— You don't really love Dad, or you wouldn't take a chance like that.

But now his sharper self had gone too far, and with a grimace Tom left the gallery, and, still in his socked feet, padded out into the concourse and up the wide marble stairs to the upper floor.

The stairs curved around the angle of the northwest corner of the concourse, and there was a place halfway up where he could stand, his eyes just level with the upper floor, and look through the marble bannisters straight into the entrance of the big gallery, the area that lay directly above the Blackfoot gallery.

To his right was the entrance to the small special exhibits room where the Mexican gold figures were on display. From this angle he couldn't see in at all. He couldn't hear anything either.

To his left the lounge area, connecting the two upstairs wings of the museum, was lit by floor to ceiling windows to north and south. There was enough light coming in for Tom to see that there was nobody there, nobody out in the open at any rate. If someone should be crouching behind a potted plant or one of the big sofas, well, that was another thing.

He'd have to take the risk. He couldn't lurk on the stairs all night. Quietly, keeping low, he padded up the remaining stairs and scudded quietly across the open area to the gallery entrance. He stopped for a minute, crouched behind a Victorian player piano, to get his bearings.

Everything was still. Softly he padded back to the entrance and looked cautiously around to his left. There was a light in the special exhibits room. He could see shadows moving on the far wall and hear indistinct voices.

He swallowed and retreated. The thieves were still there at work, then. Up to this minute none of it had been quite real. Now it was. The light and the voices made it so. Real, too, must be the SOS he'd heard tapped out on the heating pipe.

He faced the dark gallery, his flashlight held low in the palm of his hand, so that only a very little light came out from between his fingers. Round to the right, the way he'd gone in the Blackfoot gallery downstairs. He thought for just a second that he'd heard tapping when he first entered the gallery, but if he had, it had stopped now. He had nothing to guide him but the memory of where the heating pipe had vanished into the ceiling of the room below.

To the left now. Something moved almost under his feet. He jumped back and shone the flashlight low. It was real all right. No ghosts this time. Huddled against the wall, his arms fastened behind his back, was another of the security guards.

In a flash Tom was kneeling beside him, all thought of discovery gone, carefully peeling the adhesive plaster off the man's face. The guard gasped as the ripping plaster caught the hairs on his mouth and cheeks. He licked his lips. "God, Gerry, what took you so long? . . . Who? . . . You're not Gerry! Who the hell are you?" He whispered painfully, so low that Tom had to bend down to catch the man's words.

Tom shook his head impatiently. "Never mind." The guard's wrists were fastened together with a pair of solid-looking handcuffs that had been slipped around the hot-water pipe where it entered the radiator. "I can't get you out of this," Tom whispered hoarsely. "Any idea where the key is?"

"How should I know? For God's sake keep your voice down. They're still here." The man gasped as if in pain.

"I know. I saw." Tom shone the light on the man's face. Beads of sweat stood out on his forehead, and his face was grey and lined. "What should I do?"

"Get out of here as fast as you can and phone the police. Be careful. They're armed and dangerous."

"I know." Tom thought of the man lying in the downstairs gallery, the back of his head sticky with blood. "How many guards are there?"

"Four of us. God knows what's happened to the

others. They jumped me just after the lights went out."

"Do you know how many of *them* there are?"

The man shook his head. "I never saw them." His voice faded.

"Are you hurt?"

Just . . . my hands." A faint, painful whisper.

Tom shone his flashlight, but could see nothing. The handcuffs didn't seem to be too tight. He leaned over, his hand on the pipe for balance, and nearly shouted out loud with the pain and shock. The pipe was practically red-hot. How long had the guard been imprisoned in silent agony, his wrists pushed against the pipe by the position of the handcuffs?

Tom flashed his light frantically around. The pipe was rock solid, and so were the handcuffs. What on earth could he do? In the end he peeled off his thick sports socks and pushed them carefully into the small space between the pipe and the guard's wrists.

A faint sigh told him of the man's relief. He squeezed his shoulder and padded softly out of the gallery. In the small room to his left the lights still flashed and the shadows moved against the wall, huge and distorted.

"Get out and phone," the guard had said. Softly on his bare feet Tom sped down the cold marble staircase and across the concourse to the front of the building. There must surely be a phone at the information desk. Better than going outside and trying to find a pay phone. That could take ages.

There it was. With shaking fingers he dialed 911

and waited impatiently for the operator to answer.
. . . Come on! He tapped at the button and realised
that he wasn't even getting a dial tone. He lifted
the phone off the desk and looked blankly at the
loose end of cord. These people were thorough.
Now he'd *have* to go outside, he thought, with
mixed feelings of guilt and relief.

Maybe he could ring at a neighbouring house
and ask for help. No, that was hopeless. It was the
middle of the night, and Hallowe'en. They'd just
think he was a late trick-or-treater and not even
answer the door. Hurry! He'd never felt so helpless
in his life. The seconds ticked away as he stood
there with the useless telephone in his hand.

Then he remembered the pay phone in the back
of the cloakroom area, the one Mr Miles had used
that day his class had been down at the museum.
Maybe . . . He ran through the cloakroom and
vaulted over the low counter. There it was. He
lifted the handset and listened for the dial tone. It
was all right. They were good, these thieves, but
they weren't perfect. They hadn't known about
this phone. The thought gave him sudden
courage.

He dialled 911 again and waited, his eyes on the
concourse. He couldn't see the stairs from this
angle and they could be on top of him with no
warning at all. Come on!

"Police, please," he said to the operator, and in
response to her query, "Name and address,
please?" he said almost without conscious thought,
"Security. Provincial Museum."

In a second another voice was on the line. "City

109

Police."

Tom spoke rapidly, keeping his voice low and deep. "Provincial Museum here. There's a break-in in progress. Special Features Room. The pre-Columbian gold figures. The electricity's off. No alarm system. The other guards are out of it, hurt or locked up somewhere. I don't know. Hurry it up, please."

Tom could hear the man's indrawn breath clearly. "Is there any way you can delay them?" The voice was urgent. "There's a bad fire in the refinery area, and most of our strength's standing by out there. The rest is spread over the city — mostly Hallowe'en pranksters, I suspect. We'll get the nearest cars to you as soon as we humanly can."

"Thanks. Do what you can. I'll try and keep them here." Tom rang off without giving the policeman on the other end of the line time to ask awkward questions. He felt rather pleased with himself. That touch about the "other guards" was neat. He hadn't actually told the man that he was a security guard himself, but the implication was there. They'd believe him and they'd get there as fast as they could. "As soon as we humanly can," the man had said . . . How soon was soon? If they were tied up with a big fire . . . But what could be more important than a collection of priceless art belonging to another country?

Anyway, he'd done his job. Time to get out and go home, before the police *did* arrive. Only . . . he stopped short, half-way to the front entrance. Suppose the police didn't get here in time?

Suppose the thieves got clean away with the gold? It would all be his fault, wouldn't it? It was his stupid caper, stealing the medicine bundle, that had got the story of the gold exhibit into the front page headlines where any criminal might read about it and get ideas, rather than back among the art galleries and exhibits in Saturday's Leisure Section of the paper, where it belonged. If the exhibit was really stolen it would be Tom Lightfoot's fault, every bit as much as the men who actually took it.

Tom groaned in despair. All the weight that had rolled off him in the sweat lodge rolled back on. Reluctantly he turned away from the exit and started back across the concourse. The marble was icy against his bare feet. Unwillingly he crept up the stairs again and into the big gallery. As he slipped by he saw a faint light in the special exhibits room. They were still there, all right.

He tiptoed over to the guard. "Are you okay?"

The man nodded. His face did not look as strained, though a big purple lump was beginning to show on his temple.

"I've phoned the police," Tom went on. "They can't come right away. The men are still at it in there. Why is it taking them so long?"

The man grinned faintly, "Special display cases. Unbreakable glass. It would take a jack hammer or explosives, and they can't risk that — gold's soft and the pieces are fragile. They'll be having to pick the locks."

"Will they be able to, do you think?"

"If they've got an expert. All it takes is time."

"*Time.* I wish the police would hurry."

"Better get out, son. It could be rough. I don't know what you're doing here. I don't think I want to know. But get out now, while you still can, and ... thanks."

Tom shook his head. "I can't leave. It's all my fault."

"What do you mean?" The man's voice was suddenly sharp. "You're not in with *them?*"

"'Course not! It's just that ... well, I did something wrong that got the museum in the news, and there was a front page write-up on the Mexican exhibit. If that article gave them the idea then it's my fault, and I'm just as responsible as they are."

"Forget it. You're barking up the wrong tree, son. This wasn't planned in a moment. And it's too late to cry now anyway."

"I'm not crying. I'm thinking. If I could only create some sort of diversion. Just to distract them for a few minutes, delay them till the police get here."

"You keep out of their way, boy. This isn't a game."

"I know it." The image of the crumpled guard downstairs came into Tom's mind. Was he still alive? He pushed the memory resolutely away and tiptoed around the corner to the front of the gallery. There was enough light coming in from the lounge windows to illuminate the displays near the gallery entrance, though the rest were swallowed in darkness.

It's not a *game,* the man had said. Well, maybe it

should be. There they all were, juke boxes, player piano, music boxes, all the noisy antique paraphernalia. Tom tiptoed back to the guard, an idea budding hopefully in his mind.

"A couple of weeks ago our class came here and you had the music things playing. Could I get them to work now?"

"You *could*. But . . ."

"Trust me. Please. How do they work?"

"They're on battery power — too much fuss with different transformers otherwise. It just takes a key to start them."

"Where?"

"On my ring. Left hand pants pocket." The guard moved stiffly until Tom could get the keyring out. "The big square one that doesn't look like a key at all. The slots are in the back. You'll just have to look. Shove in the key and lift. That's all there is to it. Do you really know what you're doing? Be careful. Don't let them see you."

Tom nodded. Then he had a sudden worry and turned back. "What about you? Will you be all right?"

"Sure. I'll play dead if they come in here. Don't worry. I think you're crazy, but . . . good luck!"

Tom found the right key and padded off barefoot down the gallery. He decided to leave the music boxes alone. There wouldn't be time to start everything, and their sound was too delicate for the effect he wanted. Instead he switched on the player piano and the peculiar display labelled *An animated orchestra*. It contained violins, drums, cymbals and a tambourine.

Before the first whir had died away Tom was out of the gallery and hiding behind a huge philodendron in the upstairs lounge. Out there he could see what the thieves did, and if they *should* catch sight of him he had a choice of two staircases as escape routes. He was as safe as houses.

The first refined tinkle of the player piano would hardly have disturbed a sleeping canary, but when the animated orchestra joined in, the noise was wonderful. The drum banged, the cymbals clanged, the tambourine shook like a demented seance, and the violins wailed like banshees. The fact that the piano was playing a different melody certainly didn't hurt the over all effect.

"What the hell?" Three bulky shadows erupted from the special exhibits room, flashlights waving like searchlights in all directions. Tom crouched in the corner between the plant pot and the wall, his heart thumping more loudly than the drum.

"That damn guard must have got loose," one of the men muttered and vanished into the gallery. He was back in a few seconds. "No, he's out cold. You hit too hard, Charlie. You've got no finesse. I hope for your sake you haven't killed him."

"No way!" Charlie's denial was violent.

"You'd better be right," The third voice was quiet, an educated voice "Go check on the other three guards, George."

"Yes, Boss." The first man's voice was subdued. He clattered down the stairs, his big flashlight like a car's headlights in front of him.

The other two remained standing in the

doorway of the special exhibits room while the extraordinary noise went on in the main gallery. Tom began to have a strange feeling that the third man, the boss, *knew* he was there, that he was just waiting for him to make a move. His legs twitched with the terrible need to be up and running. It didn't matter where . . . just running.

Deliberately he made himself relax and tried to remember the lesson Great-grandfather had taught him. "Watch the small animals," he had said. "Face your enemy. Lie low and make your muscles soft."

Tom felt as if he had been crouching there for hours. At last steps sounded in the concourse below. Charlie and the boss moved forward out of the shadow of the doorway.

"George?" The voice echoed down the stair well.

"It's okay, Boss. The two guards I locked in the closet are still there. I could hear them swearing."

"Any way they could get out?"

"Not a chance."

"And the fourth guard?"

"Out cold on the floor of the gallery, just where Charlie left him."

Tom saw the thin shadow that was the boss raise his arm. Look at his watch. "Come on. We're running out of time. There's no one here. How long, George?"

"They're tricky locks." George sounded defensive. "Maybe a couple more minutes."

"Then get going!"

Let's get out while we're ahead, eh?" Charlie's

voice was high with panic.

"Forget it!" The thin man's voice had a knife edge to it. "That last case George is working on — I can get a million dollars from a private collector for the masks alone."

"A million . . ." Fat Charlie's voice faded. The thin man slapped him on the back and together they returned to the little room. Tom gave them thirty seconds headway and then nipped across the intervening space and turned off the music.

The silence was almost as shocking as the noise had been. It brought all three men out again, Charlie leading.

"Boss, there's *got* to be someone up here."

"George checked the guards. It's nothing . . . a timed mechanism, something like that."

"But . . ."

"Shut up and get back to wrapping the pieces. Doug will be here in exactly one minute with the van."

Tom waited until they had settled back to work. He could see their shadows, humped monstrously against the ceiling and walls, as they moved to and fro, wrapping the gold and stowing it in big suitcases. Then he turned on the big nickelodeon. It was even more raucous than the other two instruments put together. It brought all three men out of the room and into the big gallery.

"It *has* to be the guard."

"He's cuffed to the radiator. Who the hell d'you think he is — Houdini?" George's voice rose, and the thin man cut through it quietly.

"We'll check."

All three of them clattered down the gallery, their flashlights making enormous shadows on walls and ceilings. Tom padded to the entrance in his bare feet and listened. They were out of sight, but he could hear their angry voices even above the din of the nickelodeon.

"What's that round his wrists? Socks! What are you playing at, Charlie?"

"*I* didn't put them there, honest."

"Then who the hell did?"

"Maybe the guard?"

"Oh, sure! Now he's a contortionist. Anyway, he's still got his socks and shoes on."

"Well, I didn't do it."

Pause. Tom held his breath, ready to run.

"I told you to tape his mouth, Charlie."

"I did, Boss. I swear I did."

"He's right." George's deeper voice echoed. "It's here, on the floor."

Pause. Tom's heart thudded.

"There *has* to be someone in here, Boss."

"It's haunted." Charlie's voice rose. "This place gives me the creeps. Let's get out of here."

"Shut up, Charlie. Ghosts don't wear socks . . . white Adidas with blue stripes."

"Joggers wear them," George put in.

"And *kids*."

The voice was as soft as velvet, but the ice in it sent Tom bolting for the stairs. He had jumped the first three steps when he heard feet echoing on the marble below and saw the gleam of a flashlight.

The police at last, he thought thankfully, and leaned over to yell, "Hoy, up here!"

117

The flashlight caught him in a dazzle and glare. He heard a man's voice. "That you, Boss? The van's ready and waiting. HEY . . .!"

Tom stumbled back up the stairs as the man's yell brought the other three thundering out of the gallery. He sprinted across the fifty feet of carpeted lounge and into the maze of rooms in the other wing. Desperately he tried to remember the lay-out. Past the geology and the palaeontology sections was the natural history gallery. It made a complete loop that led back into the main gallery. Could he lose them in there? With three of them after him with big flashlights, and another man downstairs guarding the staircases?

Blindly he ran past the dinosaurs and into a dead end. The room that he remembered behind the dinosaurs was now closed off, probably while they prepared a new exhibit. In a blind panic he shinned up the rough back of a duck-billed dinosaur. It was only a fibre-glass model, he remembered, and prayed that it would be sturdy enough to hold his weight.

He moulded himself to the shape of its back and lay still as the clattering footsteps came closer. He shut his eyes against the reflection of the man's flashlight, praying that the dinosaur shadow on the wall behind him wouldn't look too unnatural. Maybe the man wouldn't know much about the shape of dinosaurs anyway.

Behind his eyelids it became dark again. Tom let out his breath cautiously and opened his eyes. It was all right. But only for a moment. When they didn't find him anywhere else in the gallery they'd be back for a more thorough search. And there was no way he could slip by them. They'd be bound to have a man at the gallery entrance, like a cork in a bottle. Charlie probably, the one with the heavy hand. And even if he could slip by him, how was he to get downstairs with the new man, Doug, down on the lower floor?

He could kick himself. Why had he never thought of the possibility of a fourth man? That was the reason for the open door, of course. No reason to leave it open otherwise. From inside the museum they could walk out any way they pleased. They'd even told him. "Doug'll be here with the van," they had said. Stupid, thought Tom savagely, as he flashed his inadequate light cautiously around the room. He'd made one bad choice after another. And now he was stuck. If only he could find a safe hiding place. He *must*. What was that in the side wall, close by him? A crack. It looked like a crack. Could it be a door?

He slid down off the dinosaur and went close to investigate. He was in luck. It seemed to be some kind of service door, set flush and painted the same flat black as the wall. It showed only the faintest crack from above, and there was a keyhole. No knob. Just a keyhole.

For a second Tom panicked. He could hear distant steps and voices. They were getting louder. Then he remembered the keyring that the guard had given him. There were four keys on the ring. Eliminating the music display one, that left three. One was obviously too large. His hand shook as he tried the second. It slipped in easily, but it wouldn't turn. Maybe it was just stiff. Damn! For a horrible instant it stuck and he thought he wasn't going to be able to get it out.

The third key went in like a hot knife into butter, and he was through the door in the instant before the big flashlight lit up the room again. The spring lock gave the faintest click as he pulled the door gently to behind him.

"What was that?" He heard Charlie's voice on the other side, muffled by the door.

"What the hell's the matter with you, Charlie? Afraid the Hallowe'en goblins'll get you?"

"Shut up, George. I'm sick of your lip. I heard something."

"Look around. There's nothing in here. Unless you heard that nasty thing up there gnashing its teeth, eh, Charlie?"

"Forget it, you two. We've got three million dollars worth of gold to haul down to the van."

"Suppose he gets out and calls the cops?"

"Doug won't let him by. Doug's got a gun."

"Suppose he's out already . . . he could have seen us, you know."

"In the dark?"

"But . . ."

"He's just a scared kid on a Hallowe'en caper. Even if he talked nobody'd believe him. Get moving, Charlie . . ."

Their voices faded. Tom let out his breath in a long trembling sigh. That had been too close by half. And the man called Doug who'd nearly caught him had a gun. If he'd been down those stairs a second sooner . . .

The guard had been right all along. "Get out," the man had told him. "It could be rough."

Only now it was too late to get out. Where was he anyway? His fading flashlight showed him a dusty passage with a flight of stairs leading up to his left. Since there was nowhere else to go he went up them. The flight finished in another door which opened with the same key. As Tom stepped boldly forward he suddenly saw, almost level with his eyes, the starry sky, and he felt the night wind cutting cold at his face.

In that terrifying second he remembered *Kidnapped*, and how David Balfour had climbed the Tower at his uncle's bidding, only to find the steps suddenly stop, leaving him at the edge of a precipice, one foot away from death five storeys below. David had been in the dark too.

Tom shivered and drew back his foot. He switched on the little flashlight again. It was getting very feeble. Even the starlight seemed stronger. But it was all right. He was just being silly. There was no yawning gulf in front of him, only a perfectly ordinary expanse of flat gravelled roof. There was a parapet about two feet high all round, just the right height for tripping over, he warned himself, and decided to stay well back.

The view was fantastic once he got over his squeamish feelings about height. He could see the lights of Second Avenue strung out like diminishing beads in both directions. To his right was the dark fold of trees that marked the upper slope of the ravine. Beyond it was the loom of light that was downtown. It must be very late. The apartments and houses were almost all in darkness. It was very cold now, and the moon was well up over his shoulder.

A flashing red light came along the avenue and crossed the bridge over the ravine. There was a second behind it and then a third. Tom dropped to his knees and leaned over the parapet. Two of the cars swept around the museum driveway to the front of the building. The third parked close to the entrance and Tom saw two men run to the north side of the museum.

He grinned with relief. The thieves and the priceless gold figures were still inside. The rest was up to the police. He'd done his bit. He was off the hook.

But not off the roof! He gulped. How in the world was he going to get off the roof without being detected?

Chapter Eight

Tom looked around. He could see the whole roof quite clearly in the moonlight now. It was like the top of a huge hollow box. The sides were the east and west galleries, the north must be the workrooms, while the south side was the roof of the upstairs lounge. Within the box was the enclosed courtyard that opened off the main floor concourse. It lay a sheer and dizzy forty feet below him.

To the south of the main building, beyond the room of the lounge, was the entrance area, only one storey high, but still a big drop, at least twenty-five feet from where he was. In any case it, and the roof of the Archives building which butted onto the southwest corner of the museum, were both in full view of the floor to ceiling windows of the lounge.

Up on the roof itself the only hiding place was the small box-like structure in which the staircase was concealed. It was about ten feet square and Tom guessed that it must also contain the inspection area for the mechanism of the elevator that was used by staff personnel and by handicapped visitors to the museum.

Perhaps there was some way he could get in and hide on top of the elevator. He'd seen it done on television often enough. But the thought of the height and the idea of being trapped in a small dark space turned his stomach. "I'd rather be caught," he said aloud.

Maybe he'd be safe if he waited up here until everyone had left. The door leading up from the dinosaur gallery was locked, after all, and so was the one at the top of the stairs. If the police caught all three men — no, it was four, wasn't it, counting the man with the van — why should they bother to search the roof?

Tom wondered how much the guard had told the cops about him. His socks were on the scene as evidence and he had the guard's keys. There wasn't much he could do about the socks — and he'd have some explaining to do to Mother about them — but if he could just get rid of the keys the police might believe he'd left, the way the guard had told him to.

Down in the grass so they wouldn't be damaged, but hopefully where they'd soon be found, that was the thing to do. He crawled across to the eastern side of the roof, hating the height and the lowness of the parapet. The wind was strong, smelling of winter, and it buffetted his back as if it *wanted* to push him over. Below him was grass and beyond the grass the driveway, where the police car was parked. Where the side of the museum was floodlit the grass was a brilliant patch of green in the surrounding darkness. Carefully he tossed the heavy key ring into the middle of the bright patch. With luck they'd find it and surmise that he'd left that way, tossing the keys as he ran. Then they wouldn't bother about him any more.

He backed thankfully away from the edge. Gosh, heights were horrible. To think that some people actually climbed mountains for the fun of it! The gravel cut his feet. Now that the excitement was wearing off he noticed the pain, and the cold too. He sat down with his back against the outbuilding and warmed them with his hands — though they weren't that hot either — and put his runners back on. If only he had his socks . . .

A siren wail tore through the night and Tom scrambled to his feet, balancing against the buffeting wind. An ambulance swung past the police car and around the driveway to the front. With an odd lurch in his stomach Tom crossed the roof and crouched down at the south edge, looking over the parapet and beyond the roof of the entrance area to the paved terrace and the wide stairs beyond it.

Two attendants hurried in, a folded stretcher between them. Tom waited. His mouth felt dry. Suppose the first guard was dead? In some way he'd feel responsible . . . always wonder whether there was something he should have done . . . if he should have called for help sooner . . . if he'd never started this caper . . .

When the men came out again, the stretcher between them, Tom could see the man's face above the enveloping blankets. They'd cover his face if he were dead, he told himself, and sighed with relief. The second guard came down the steps, supported by one of the policemen, and the ambulance took off, its siren wailing, around the curve of the driveway by the Archives. The other two guards must be all right then. And nobody was dead.

The sound of voices and shoe leather on pavement made him look down again from his dizzy viewpoint. Four men were coming down the steps, handcuffed in pairs, a covey of police around them. He could see the tops of their heads, perfectly ordinary heads. From this height you could only tell the cops from the robbers by the uniform caps. Funny, they didn't look like anybody particular. He'd never know them in a crowd. Tom felt he knew more about the men from listening to them talk in the dark than he'd ever find out from seeing them face to face.

The prisoners were pushed into the two police cars and driven off. It became very quiet again. There must be two guards left in the museum now, and two policemen. The lights were still off, so presumably the alarm system wasn't working either. How long would it take to fix? If the wires had been cut they'd have to send for a City Power crew, probably not till morning.

If he were going to slip down the staircase and escape from inside the museum, now would be the time to do it, before the alarms were reconnected and the whole place lit up like a Christmas tree again . . . Only he'd thrown away the keys. He could get back in by turning the latch on his side of the doors, but once they were shut behind him, that would be that. He'd have burned his bridges.

He sat down on the roof close to the parapet, to think about it, in a spot which gave him a good view of the whole lounge area, the only place in the museum with windows, the only place where he could actually see what was going on inside. He watched patiently for half an hour. He saw the movements of flashlights on the stairs, crossing and recrossing the lounge, vanishing into the galleries at either end. He saw glimpses of light in the lower concourse, but he couldn't tell for sure where all the guards and police were at any given moment. Only that they were searching the entire building. The chance of getting out unnoticed was too small to be worth betting on.

Tom went back to the outbuilding which housed the staircase top and the elevator machinery, and sat down with his back against the south wall. It was a little warmer out of the wind, and after a few minutes he became aware of an occasional puff of warm air from a ventilator grille just above his head. It wasn't much, but compared with the rest of the roof it was Hawaii.

From his vantage point he could see the whole skein of river, silver in the moonlight, curling across the dark tree-clad valley below him. The moon was near setting. Above him was the crooked W of Cassiopeia. Close by was Andromeda.

Gosh, he felt tired all of a sudden, as if he'd been wound up with a rubber band that had suddenly come loose and lost all its zing. He leaned back and stared up at the sky. On a clear night like this he ought to be able to make out the galaxy of Andromeda . . . he'd got sharp eyes — Indian eyes. Was it that small star smudge there? Two million years ago, when the sloth and the hairy mammoth roamed Earth, long before Man came on the scene, the tiny smudge of light he was looking at had just left their twin galaxy. Two million years . . .

How many planets were up there in that other galaxy, Tom wondered. As many as ours? Twice as many? And how many of those planets would have intelligent beings? . . . Beings who might, right now, be sitting on a roof under a night sky, looking up at the faint star that was really the whole Milky Way galaxy, and thinking, two million years ago . . .

Above Tom's head the stars seemed to spin and drop away into the infinity of expanding space. He felt like a tiny speck of dust on the surface of that minuscule collection of coagulated star particles called Earth. Tinier and tinier until he vanished altogether.

When Tom woke up the moon had set and it was very dark. He was cold, colder than he'd ever been in his life. He felt chilled right through to the bone. His bare ankles were like boney icicles and when he tried to move he found he was as stiff as a winter's wash. He breath came short in smoky puffs and his lips and cheeks were stiff and numb.

It was quiet, so quiet that for a second Tom wondered if he'd suddenly gone deaf, until he heard the stiffened material of his jeans rub against itself as he tried to straighten his legs. Close to his ear was an echoing rustle, and he moved suddenly, starled. What was it, a bird? Or a mouse? He shone his flashlight on the air vent at his back, saw a brown furry bundle move, and caught it gently in his hand.

It was a bat. Looking back afterwards he wondered why he hadn't yelled out loud and dropped the thing. He'd always hated bats. But there was a strange accepting kind of magic about this lonely roof top under the starlit sky. He sat comfortably, his back against the wall, his flashlight in his lap, his hands cupping the small furry body.

Carefully he straightened out the big leathery wings, felt the matchstick-thin brittle bones, the fingernails at the edges. He stroked its brown fur with one finger, and the small creature's mouth opened in squeaky protest. He had a glimpse of a rose-pink tongue and small needle-sharp teeth.

Were there creatures something like this on some planet in Andromeda, Tom wondered. Or, who knows, perhaps the 'men' up there looked like bats themselves. What was it thinking, sitting huddled in his hands? It was so tiny that he could crush it just by squeezing his hand shut. It seemed so vulnerable, and yet he knew that there had been bats around since pre-historic times, since the light of Andromeda that he was seeing had started in its journey to Earth. There were bats everywhere in the world. They ate insects, pollen, nectar, fruit, animals, blood, whatever they could find. They had adapted. They survived.

"Oh, bat, are you my spirit?" Tom spoke out loud, stroking the fine brown fur. "You are such a mixture of opposites. Mammal with wings, bird with warm blood and fur. You are shy and quiet and yet you prosper. You follow your own path and never get lost, even in the dark. You *must* be my spirit."

The bat's mouth opened in another inaudible

squeak. Carefully Tom folded its wings close to its body, and hung it upside down by its clawed feet to one of the bars of the warm-air grille. The bat shifted, refolded its wings and went back to sleep.

Tom got up slowly. In a light-headed trance born of hunger, cold and excitement he walked stiffly across the roof. In the museum below all was quiet. No lights showed in the lounge area. The last police car had gone. He walked the whole length of the building from east to west, sure-footed and unafraid, until he was standing at the south-west corner. Twenty feet below him was the roof of the Archives building.

Without any hesitation he climbed over the parapet, hung by his fingers and dropped quietly through the darkness to the roof below. He landed softly, springing on toes and knees, absorbing the shock without conscious thought or effort.

Looking at the building later in daylight he shuddered at the drop, but that night some strange magic seemed to be in charge of his body and he could do nothing wrong. From the roof of the Archives it was a simple slide, and then a drop to the flower bed below, empty now and soft, its soil turned over, ready for Spring.

Without fear or subterfuge Tom walked across the grass and out of the museum grounds. He walked through the dreaming streets meeting nobody on his way home. The house was sleeping. The window above the back porch was open two inches, just as he had left it. He climbed up the trellis, pushed it up and clambered in. He remembered to pull off his runners, and then he fell into bed, pushing aside the rolled-up blanket that he'd put there all those hours before, unaware of cold or hunger, only of the need for sleep.

On Thursday morning Tom managed to scramble out of bed just before his mother came in to call him. He was standing blinking at the window in his crumpled jeans and roll-neck when she opened the door. "Oh, are you up and dressed already, dear? Early bird. I'll go down and get your breakfast."

When she'd safely gone, he stumbled into the bathroom, stripped off his soiled clothes and showered. He was filthy, especially his feet. He flung on clean clothes and clattered downstairs when Mother called, "Breakfast's ready."

It was a sunny morning and his parents' mood seemed to reflect it. Mother was singing over the coffee, and Father actually kissed her as he left. "Keep your fingers crossed, Carol. I heard on the grapevine that the new appointments to the bench will be announced today."

Pete was lurking outside school when Tom showed up. "Did you listen to the radio?" he asked without preamble.

Tom shook his head.

"The museum was burgled last night. Four men broke in and tried to rip off those pre-Columbian figures. And, as if you didn't know, someone phoned the police and tippd them off, someone inside. Tom, it was you, wasn't it?"

"Was it me what?"

"*You* know." Pete looked over his shoulder. The school steps were crowded.

"Maybe." Tom hedged.

"I knew it had to be you. Lord, what luck!" Pete's voice rose excitedly. Tom nudged him and he whispered. "The announcer said that the police caught the thieves red-handed and got back all the gold figures safely, thanks to this anonymous tip-off. He said that the Mexican Government is offering a reward. You're going to claim it, of course."

"No *way!*"

Pete stared. "Why on earth not? You're crazy, Tom! Think about it. It's bound to be a lot of money . . . gosh, even a thousandth of the value of that gold would be worth having." Pete's clever eyes shone.

Tom suddenly found himself wondering what he'd thought was so special about Pete, what he'd envied. He was a nice enough guy and a good friend, but he really wasn't all that great. "I'd have to tell them what I was doing there, wouldn't I?" he explained carefully. "And I'd no right to be in the museum at all at that hour of the night."

"The newscast said that one of the guards had talked to a boy. He guessed that he'd slipped into the museum for a Hallowe'en prank."

"But we know that's not true, don't we?"

"Oh, for goodness sake, you could go along with it, couldn't you? It wouldn't hurt anyone."

"I'm sick and tired of lies, Pete. There have been too many lies in this business already. I don't want anything more to do with it. It's all over. Finished."

"You're crazy," Pete said flatly. "I'd claim the

money myself if I thought I could get away with it. After all . . .''

"Go ahead." Tom shrugged. "But you're on your own."

"You're a great friend! There's got to be a catch . . . they wouldn't advertise the reward money like that unless there was a way of proving who the informant was. You must have done something out of the way, besides just phoning in the warning . . . I suppose you wouldn't tell me . . .''

"No."

Pete stared at him, and Tom stared right back. Pete's eyes were the first to drop. "Oh, well." He shrugged and sighed dramatically. "Easy come. Easy go. But it does seem a shocking waste of perfectly good money. Come on, fellow, there's the bell."

Chapter Nine

On Sunday morning Tom and Dad were eating an early breakfast of waffles and syrup in peaceful amity. Mother hadn't come down yet to start the weekly argument about Tom's visit to his great-grandfather. Suddenly the peace was shattered by a series of rattles and bangs that came steadily closer and closer.

"What on earth?" Dad got to his feet just as Mother came into the breakfast room in a rustle of housecoat. She went to the window and pulled back the glass curtain.

"Mark, do look. The tackiest old car. Gracious, I do believe it's going to fall apart right in front of our house. Can't you do something? Make him move on, dear, or give him a push or something. Anything. Oh, what a racket!"

"Good lord!" Dad peered over her shoulder. "Carol, it's the old man."

"Mark, it can't be!"

"But it *is*. I wonder what on earth he's doing here."

"Mark, I'm not dressed. The house is a mess after the party last night, and Gertrude won't be in till tomorrow. Oh, it's all too tiresome. He's going to stay for lunch, I know it. Why couldn't he at least have warned us he was coming? With you at the golf course all day and Tom out I hadn't planned a *thing* for lunch. Why couldn't he have *phoned*?"

"He doesn't have a phone, you know that. Stop fussing. Carol. You'll manage. What about me? I'm supposed to tee off at ten with Judge Bates. As a future colleague it's even more important for me to keep everything sweet."

"You could phone and cancel, I suppose." Mother ran her hand through her hair. "Oh, why doesn't that awful noise *stop*?"

"At this hour? And what would I say. 'Pardon me, Judge, but my old grandfather just dropped in unannounced off the reservation.' Just great! Terrific! Any other ideas, dear?"

"Mark, don't pick at me like that."

Tom gulped down his milk and shot out of the door in the middle of the argument.

"Hey, Great-grandfather!"

"Morning, Tom."

Tom put his hands on the frame of the car door and grinned. The old man smiled slowly back. He sat tranquilly at the wheel while around him the car shook and trembled and a haze of blue smoke rose.

"You need a new muffler, Great-grandfather."

"Oh, this one's good for a few miles yet."

"Really, though. You could die some winter day with the windows up and all that stuff coming inside the car. Buy a new muffler and I'll help you install it. I've done it in automotives in school, and I know exactly how it goes."

"Maybe I'll do that, boy."

Mother and Father came down the garden path in a flurry of exlamations of surprise. On Mother's pale cheeks two red spots of vexation burned like badly put-on rouge. Tom saw the drapes of the houses across the road tremble, and knew that she was aware of it too. It made him want to laugh, and yet he was sorry for Mother at the same time.

"Aren't you going to come into the house, Great-grandfather?" he suggested.

"No, thank you, boy. I have an appointment. I just came to pick you up, if you're ready. Then afterwards we'll drive home to spend the day together as usual."

"Sure." Tom valuted into the old jalopy.

"Tom, your hair! Your coat! Wait a moment," Mother wailed. Then, turning on the path, "You'll come back here ... for lunch ... won't you, Grandfather?" Mother's cordiality came out in little forced spurts, like sharp beads on a string.

Great-grandfather shook his head gently. "I'll take Tom right back with me after I've talked to this man. Will you pick him up at the usual time this evening, Mark?"

"Yes, sir, of course. You're sure you wouldn't like to come back here?"

The old chief smiled his slow gentle smile. "Go play your golf, grandson. I hope it all turns out to be worth your while."

He put the car in gear. It jerked suddenly forward and stopped dead with a sudden grinding noise as if something had fallen out. Mother came hurrying out of the house with Tom's rawhide jacket, the first thing she'd grabbed from the hall closet, Tom knew. She'd never have picked it out deliberately. "Tom, you should *think*. It's a lovely morning, but it *is* November. By mid afternoon it'll be freezing."

The car started up again, and this time Great-grandfather managed to keep it going. He chugged very carefully down the middle of the street. Luckily there was very little other traffic this early on Sunday morning. They crossed the main road and turned left on to Second Avenue.

It was horribly familiar territory. "Great-grandfather!" Tom's voice suddenly rose and cracked. "Where are you going?"

"To the museum," Great-grandfather answered calmly and swung the old car in through the gate marked 'Out'. He pulled up in front of the side door to the Archives and switched off the engine.

"We can't go in here. Who do you want to see? It's not even open till one o'clock on Sundays."

"Then it's lucky I have an arrangement to meet someone, isn't it?"

"Who? Who are you meeting? Why? Great-grandfather, it's not funny! Why are you smiling like that?"

"Be still, son. You are talking like a man with too much on his conscience. Be still. I am meeting a Mr Erickson. He is an archivist. Do you know what that is?"

Tom shook his head. "Something to do with old papers and things, I think," he said vaguely.

"Then everything should be clear to you. He came out to the reservation to talk to me last Thursday."

Tom stared. Great-grandfather sat relaxed, his hands resting lightly on the wheel.

"Well?" Tom's voice rose.

"Well, what? You wish to know what we talked about? To tell you that would take as long as it took us to talk and he stayed with me the whole day. I had things to tell him about our ceremonies, and he ... ah, for a young man, he had much knowledge to share in return. It was a good meeting." He lapsed into silence again.

Tom looked round. The big parking lot was empty. The museum had a closed and deserted look. "Great-grandfather, are you *sure* your appointment was for today?"

"Oh, yes, I am sure."

"What time?"

"Nine o'clock."

"Nine? But it's only a few minutes after eight now. We've ages to wait!"

"It is a good day for waiting. See how the sun warms the stones in front of us, and there is no wind."

"That's true enough. But why on earth did you have to get here so early?" Tom realised suddenly that he was starting to sound just like Dad, and he bit his lip and stopped talking.

"I was not sure how many times the car would break down on the way here, and I wished to be on time. It is a special occasion."

"What occasion?"

But Great-grandfather pretended not to hear, and Tom had nothing to do but sit back and try and not fidget while the minutes drowsed by.

Eventually a car pulled up neatly in the parking stall next to theirs and a man got out. The 'young man' was a scholarly looking fifty. He shook hands with Great-grandfather and then leaned over to shake hands with Tom, too.

"So you're young Mr Lightfoot, the great-grandson, eh?"

"Yes, sir. I'm Tom Lightfoot."

"Come in, both of you. Chief, I have it all ready. I was able to complete the formalities yesterday as I promised." He unlocked an unexpected door in the end wall of the Archives, ushered them both inside and down a cream-painted corridor to a small office, stacked with files, boxes and folders.

"Take a seat, won't you?" He bustled about, dumping the contents of two chairs on to an already stacked table. He himself perched on the corner of the desk, swinging one leg. "Sorry for the mess. I've got behind, what with one thing and another. Quite a stir that affair made the other night. It had us all hopping the next day."

Tom felt himself flinch and tried to keep his voice casual. "The burglary, you mean? How are the two guards, do you know?"

"The guards? Ah, yes. One of them was released the next day. The other had a severe concussion, but I believe he is doing quite well now."

"That's good," Tom muttered and stared at the floor.

"Before I give it to you..." Mr Erickson suddenly jumped down from his perch on the desk. "I'd like to show you the display case. I think you'll approve, Chief Lightfoot. I hope so. This way, if you will follow me."

He led them briskly down the corridor and through a swing door. They were suddenly back on familiar territory. Tom recognised the entrance to the cafeteria, with the concourse beyond it.

"Upstairs." The archivist's voice echoed in the empty building. He pointed. "Upstairs was where all the fun and games went on the other night. Hallowe'en, eh? Quite a stir it made. Only excitement the museum's seen in its life, so far — since we had royalty to open it, that is."

Tom looked at the ground, afraid that the little man could read his guilty mind. The archivist led them to the Blackfoot gallery. "Around to your right, Chief Lightfoot, this way. You know your way around here, of course, Tom."

Tom shied like a spooked horse. "What? Why do you say that?"

"Didn't your class visit the museum a few weeks ago?"

"Yes, of course, I forgot," Tom muttered, feeling his neck and ears grow hot.

They followed the archivist to the display case from which Tom and Pete had stolen the medicine bundle. Tom had the crazy feeling that the case must be covered with enormous visible finger-prints, all of them his, and that in the middle of his forehead there was probably a sign flashing on and off like neon ... guilty ... guilty ... guilty.

"Well?" Mr̄ Erickson's quiet voice interrupted. "Notice anything different?"

Tom blinked and stared. "It's gone again! I mean ..." Too late he realised his mistake. He floundered on. "I mean, wasn't there another bundle, over there, in the corner." He pointed. He could see his hand trembling and he shoved it in his pocket.

"Quite right. You have a good memory. You may notice that the original card has been replaced by another. Perhaps you would like to read it aloud to your great-grandfather. The printing is rather small for this light."

Tom stared blankly at Mr Erickson and then bent obediently over the case and read aloud. "This case originally held a Blackfoot Ghost Bundle, believed to be the last still in existence. It has been returned to Chief Samuel Lightfoot on extended loan, for ceremonial purposes."

Tom's voice faltered. He looked up into the bespectacled grey eyes of the little archivist. "I don't understand."

"I explained to the Chief when I talked to him earlier that the museum authorities would have preferred to return the bundle to his band as an outright gift. However, since it was deeded in good faith by its last owner to the people of Alberta through the Provincial Museum, the legal red tape involved in reversing this bequest would be so horrendous and time-consuming that we arrived at the above formula as a compromise. You might be interested to know that we are getting in touch with other bands who may want the return of various ceremonial and religious objects. This," he tapped the case, "this is only the beginning." He smiled.

"Don't you *mind*. I mean, I thought museum people wanted to keep things neatly in cases no matter what."

"Only when the things are past and dead. That's

what museums like this one are for — memories that might otherwise be lost for ever. But if something is still being used and is still alive in people's minds and hearts, then it has no place in a museum. If you wonder why I'm so cheerful about it, it's because I'm not the loser. I resorted to a little gentle blackmail and persuaded Chief Lightfoot that the very next time he holds a ghost dance he will allow me to be present. If I can put tapes and notes of the ceremony into the archives then there will never be any danger of the knowledge being lost, the way it so nearly was this time."

He smiled at them both. He was a dry little sparrow of a man, and yet Tom found himself warming to his enthusiasm. "Now," he went on. "Let us go back to my office and I will formally hand over the bundle to you, Chief Lightfoot, and take your receipt."

As they left the gallery Tom caught the eye of the TV camera high up under the ceiling. He wondered if the guard he had helped would possibly recognise him again. He felt all enormous hands and feet. He swallowed, shoved his hands into his pockets again and followed the others, trying to look nonchalant.

Back in the office Mr Erickson solemnly handed Great-grandfather the precious bundle, and solemnly and slowly Great-grandfather signed the receipt.

"Funny thing about that burglary," the archivist remarked as he showed them out. "It was well planned and executed, and yet the whole thing fell apart because of a child's prank. Nobody's turned up yet to claim the reward either. Odd, isn't it?"

"Do they have any clues?" Tom's voice cracked and he cleared his throat and repeated the question. "The police, I mean. Who the informant was and all that?"

"Nothing useful. I understand. A naked footprint in some dirt behind one of the tropical plants upstairs. Naked, I ask you! Well, the police don't have footprints on file and there's no reason to suppose that the boy had a record anyway. Then there was a pair of blue and white sports socks left at the scene. That's not much of a clue either. Everyone wears them nowadays, don't they? You're wearing them yourself, I see." His eyes twinkled as he pointed at Tom's feet. Tom's ears crimsoned and he scrambled hastily into the car.

They were out of town and driving along the highway before Tom spoke. "Do you suppose he knew it was me?"

"Of course. He is certainly not a stupid man, even if he chooses to spend his life looking after little papers."

"He did nothing about it."

"Why should he? No harm was done. As he said, one pair of socks looks much like another. Though I must admit that I am curious to know what a grandson of mine, that I've shown all the skills of the wood, should be thinking about to leave his socks behind."

Tom began to laugh. "It's a long story, Great-grandfather. One day I'll tell it to you in exchange for a new one of yours." He touched the bundle that lay on the seat between them. "So it's come home again."

"Yes. This time the right way."

"Yes. That's important. I do see that now. I couldn't before. I was so angry at you, Great-grandfather, for not appreciating my gift."

"I know you were." The old chief nodded. "One has to learn that he cannot give to others what is not truly his to give."

"You can't always tell for sure. You get muddled. I did."

"That is true. Your own self is about the only thing that you can be sure of as a gift."

They drove on to the turn-off and bumped slowly over the dirt road. The white dust rose in a cloud and mixed with the blue smoke from the exhaust.

"So you found your spirit, eh, Tom?"

"It shows, does it?" Tom found himself grinning happily.

"Like a hunter coming back to his lodge with meat. I can see it in your eyes and in the spring of your feet and the way you hold your head. How was it? Can you speak of it?"

"It was so strange. I can't put it into words properly. I'd worried so much about finding my spirit, and yet when it happened I'd forgotten that I was supposed to be looking for it. I just woke up and everything was very clear and cold and yet like a dream in spite of being very clear — do you know? — and then I found this little bat sleeping . . ."

"A bat?" Great-grandfather's eyebrows went up.

"I know." Tom began to laugh. "It's not exactly

a kosher spirit symbol for an Indian, is it? But maybe that's why it's right for me. Because I'm not a kosher Indian. But I knew I had found it."

"And what did it teach you, this spirit bat?" Great-grandfather's voice was serious, though laughter still lingered in his eyes.

"That I do belong to two worlds. And that it doesn't have to make me muddled or split down the middle. You can take black and white and mix them together and get nothing but a dingy grey, or you can keep them clean and separate and make a beautiful pattern. That's what I'm going to try and do with my life. I can't be an Indian chief. I can't be a white lawyer. I can only be *me*. I don't know just what that's going to mean yet, but I think that now I know how to listen — to myself, I mean — instead of to everybody else telling me what I ought to do." Tom put his hand on Great-grandfather's arm. "I don't know how to put it into words, but I know that it's going to be all right."

The old Indian turned the car off the road and parked. He picked up the ghost bundle carefully in both hands. In silence he and Tom walked up towards the house. At the door he stopped and held the bundle high above his head. He turned to the south and to the west and to the north and to the east. His eyes shone and he stood straight and tall.

For a moment Tom saw him as he must have been sixty years before, straight and slim and proud. Then he was just a very old stooped Indian in a shabby red mackinaw. He led the way into the house and put the bundle up on the mantel.

"Well, boy, what shall we do today?"

"Some tea first, Great-grandfather. And then let's walk through the woods to the bluffs."